Unclean Jobs
for Women and Girls

ECCO ART OF THE STORY

The Delicate Prey by Paul Bowles

Catastrophe by Dino Buzzati

The Essential Tales of Chekhov by Anton Chekhov

Whatever Happened to Interracial Love? by Kathleen Collins

Continent by Jim Crace

The Vanishing Princess by Jenny Diski

The Garden Party by Katherine Mansfield

Wild Nights! by Joyce Carol Oates

Mr. and Mrs. Baby by Mark Strand

In the Garden of the North American Martyrs by Tobias Wolff

UNCLEAN JOBS
for Women and Girls

ALISSA NUTTING

HarperCollins books may be purchased for educational, business, or sales promotional use. For information, please email the Special Markets Department at SPsales@harpercollins.com.

FIRST EDITION

Designed by Suet Yee Chong

Library of Congress Cataloging-in-Publication Data has been applied for.

ISBN 978-0-06-269985-5

18 19 20 21 22 LSC 10 9 8 7 6 5 4 3 2 1

... *her important name is I. I stand with this, and with the urgency that saying I creates, a facing up to sheer presence, death and responsibility, the potential for blowing away all the gauze.*

—Alice Notley, "The Poetics of Disobedience"

Contents

Introduction... ix

Dinner..1

Model's Assistant... 9

Porn Star..23

Zookeeper..35

Bandleader's Girlfriend................................37

Ant Colony..63

Knife Thrower..73

Deliverywoman...79

Corpse Smoker 101

Cat Owner..107

Cannibal Lover 111

Teenager..123

Hellion 133

Trainwreck..145

Gardener..149

Dancing Rat 157

Magician...169

Acknowledgments......................................173

Introduction

When I was eight years old, I became convinced aliens were coming to abduct me. The panic I experienced was all-consuming. It horrified my Catholic parents. I'm not saying they would've been *thrilled* if I'd been possessed by a demon instead, but they would've *really preferred it* to abduction anxiety. Exorcisms are on-brand with the Vatican; extraterrestrials aren't.

I felt the aliens wouldn't come to get me in daylight. I couldn't picture them, say, at our local grocery store, hiding in wait to snatch me up behind a pyramid-shaped display of tomato soup cans. Aliens struck me as being rather goth. Luckily, in the daylight, there could be no more effective goth repellent than our home's hideous furnishings. We had 1970s green and yellow linoleum floors. Neon orange and brown, scratchy, wool plaid furniture. And on the living room wall, a huge, earnest painting of two raccoons someone had made while serving a prison sentence. I'm not sure if the artist painted it for my father as a heartfelt gift or as an act of revenge. The raccoons had a very, You haven't heard the awful news yet, have you? look about them. The painting was in a direct line of sight from our front door, so upon entering the house I always looked to them first in a sort of litmus test, telepathically asking the raccoons, "How bad are things today?" We had a thermometer hanging outside the main window that my parents checked several times a day during performative arguments over who could hold out the longest before turning on the furnace. But the only forecast I worried about came from the raccoons' expressions, and their answer never changed: "Well, things are very bad."

I figured the aliens would come for me while my parents slept. Which meant I needed to stay up all night. Unfortunately I lived in a stimulant-free household, in every sense of the term. Our medicine cabinet's contents were a laminated bookmark of the Lord's Prayer and a jar of Vaseline that looked borrowed from a World War II submarine's engine room.

Exploring the house at night was too scary, and my parents would hear my footsteps. I tried to wait out the night in the bathroom once, with the door shut and the light on, but my mother found me. "Why do you think you're safe in here?" she asked. "Do aliens not go to the bathroom?" The pink foam of her rollers looked like an additional, external brain atop her scalp. She was there as a representative of logic and reason. I knew the terror I felt wasn't rational. But I couldn't stop feeling it.

I began to hallucinate from lack of sleep. The edges of my life took on an animated quality that I accepted and dismissed. Piano keys would move. Furniture sometimes appeared to be sneaking up on me when I wasn't looking at it straight on. I knew that this was my mind, that I alone was experiencing these things. I knew that about my fear, too. And other things, like my thoughts at church. I didn't have faith. But my family did, and I needed to pretend to.

I also pretended that my anxiety was getting better. My thoughts and feelings were very different from my words and actions. I experienced this disconnect as a profound loneliness. My parents named my problem "the alien thing," and I came to realize this was an apt description of me, too. I didn't seem to belong in my family. Maybe I didn't fear I was going to be abducted so much as reclaimed.

The only thing I could really do in bed all night without waking up my parents was read, and since I had no access to caffeine, I needed terror. At the library I started checking out the most frightening things possible. If the librarians inquired, I claimed the books were for an older brother, but mostly they were too scared of me to ask questions: by age nine, lack of sleep was significantly impacting my appearance. With my dark under-eye circles, gaunt face, unbrushed hair, and affected smile that tried too hard to reassure all was fine, I looked as though my parents had a shot at needing that exorcism after all.

Reading horror—and later, watching scary movies—gave me the chance to take a more objective perspective on dread. I was able to study its construction and analyze forms of fear. Horror also gave me the chance to feel understood. These were characters who knew something bad was going to happen, even if those around them didn't. When I first saw the horror movie *A Nightmare on Elm Street* at a slumber party, I was so overcome with relief that I had to sneak off to the bathroom to weep. The teenagers in the movie knew this feeling I'd been alone with for years—that if they went to sleep they were going to die. That what they were afraid of sounded too incredulous to be real. That no one was able to help or protect them.

To me, *A Nightmare on Elm Street* was more like *A Validation of Horrific Feelings I Struggled with in Isolation (on Elm Street)*.

The most frightening form of terror, I still feel, is loneliness.

Particularly the loneliness of not being believed. This is a common theme in scary films and stories: characters seek help only to be dismissed or ignored, reassured that all is well. Not only do they have to endure terror, they have to endure it all by themselves because no one will take them seriously. Oftentimes, despite knowing otherwise, they even begin to doubt themselves. They don't want to be ostracized. They don't want to be alone in belief.

This central juxtaposition of horror—denial of the truth—is also the absurdist linchpin of humor. What's more nonsensical than mistaking danger for safety? Indifference for love? Worse for better? Our confusion of the harmful for the benign is so often absurd. As is our denial of harm. Our preference of harm, our choice of harm. So often, I make terrible (and terror-driven) decisions. Sometimes they feel absurd in hindsight. Sometimes they feel absurd as I'm choosing them. Sometimes I deny their absurdity for as long as possible.

Humor and horror are both vehicles for examining the terror of loneliness, the absurdity of it. We attempt to deny terror and absurdity through order—schedules, routines, organization—and humor and horror both allow us to disrupt order and view the terror beneath. While horror tends to show this through the situational (*something* is out of order: a threat is disrupting order), humor can show this through the everyday: *existence itself,* its very basis and contents, is out of order. Death is out of order. Suffering is out of order. Pain is out of order. Humor lets us approach the spaces of terror in everyday life where order is not possible.

Similarly, short stories with fabulist, surreal, or strange premises that escape realism lift the veil of everyday order to gaze at everyday terror. What's revealed to be most surreal aren't the things that differ from reality—the odd settings or mythical beings—but the things that do not change no matter how bizarre the story's world. Such as loneliness.

Order wants to deny terror. Fabulism, absurdity, and humor are tricks against order. Humor is perhaps the most versatile of the three in terms of letting us acknowledge private pain in public. Order tells us not to be in pain in front of others, but humor lets us costume our pain for social presentation. In stories, humor can be a desperate act in the best way; it can show desperation. Humor allows us to convey terror without being shunned, and to experience terror without being isolated. Humor is a way of saying, *I'm in so much pain that I'm willing to dress it up and show it to you. Laugh with me so that I will not be alone.*

Unclean Jobs
for Women and Girls

Dinner

I am boiling inside a kettle with five other people. Our limbs are bound. Our intestines and mouths are stuffed with herbs and garlic, but we can still speak. We smell great despite the pain.

The guy next to me has a fluffy, vaguely pubic black hairdo that makes him strongly resemble Elvis. It may be the humidity.

Across the kettle a man is trying to cry, but his tears keep mixing with sweat and instead of looking sad he just seems extra warm. For a moment, I think of how extravagant it would be if we were actually boiling in tears, hundreds of thousands of them, the sweetest-true tears of infants and children, instead of in a yellowy, chickenish broth.

I am the only woman in the kettle, which strikes me as odd. I'm voluptuous and curvy; I can understand why someone would want to gobble me up. The men do not look so delicious. One, a very old man across the kettle from me, keeps drifting in and out of a semiconscious state. Whenever his head droops down toward the broth, he will suddenly, just as the tip of his nose touches one of the surface's bubbles, snap upright and utter a name. "Stanley" is the first. The second, "David." Initially we think he is saying the names of his children; we even continue to humor him after he gets to the fifteenth (perhaps he's moved on to grandchildren?), but as he yells his fortieth name it's clear that he is not being poignant. He's delirious.

"We should join him," the crying man sobs. "These are the last moments of our lives. Shouldn't we all be calling out the names of everyone we've ever met? Ever known? Ever loved?"

"Ah ha," agrees Elvis.

But the pallid man to Elvis's left is less fond of this idea. A series of teardrop tattoos on his upper cheek imply victories in multiple prison kills. Ironically, he is tied up right next to the crying man. "I like silence," the tattooed man says.

The man on my right isn't really my type. But he's smiling at me through the spices and trimmings shoved into his mouth, undeterred by them. Since we're about to be eaten, I decide, why not give this a try?

Mindful that we're pressed for time, I begin with, "I love you." It's coming from a good-pretend place. I want to pack as much into these last few moments as I can.

But when I watch the impact my words have on him, their effect is very real. Maybe, I figure, since we are all cooking toward the finish line, things *are* kind of fast-forwarding. Maybe, in this context, what I'd just said could be true.

And then it is. Seconds pass and love for him appears throughout my body and grows rapidly, like ice crystals or sea monkeys.

We stare at one another and he scoots toward me as much as our fetters will allow, enough that our fingertips can touch. "I love you, too," he says. "If we weren't tied up, I'd give you the softest kiss you've ever felt in your life, right on your steamy lips."

From the corner of my eye, I notice that the tattooed man, who up until this point hasn't been very chatty, is suddenly showing variegated upper teeth. His lips now pull back wide and verbalize the list of things he would do to me, were we not tied up. They are not romantic or legal.

"You're a monster," my lover says to him. "The rest of us shouldn't have to boil in your juices."

"Ah ha," agrees Elvis.

"We're dying all the same, just like this murderer," weeps the crying man. "It isn't fair."

The old man's head rises up. A drop of yellow broth falls from his chin. "Stella," he rasps, then his eyes roll back and his head falls down. I smile.

"That's my name!" Glee fills me though I don't know why. "He just said my name," I tell my new lover, whose fingertips squeeze my own.

"Stella." My lover whispers my name into the hot mist.

"What if it's some kind of death list," the crying man snivels. "What if that old guy's been here for ages, been in pots with hundreds of people who've all been eaten, but he always gets left behind because he's so old. It would drive a person crazy. It might make him repeat over and over again the names of people he's had to watch die in a half-hearted attempt to bring them back." After pondering this, the crying man lets out a long, shrill sob that is chirp-like. It reminds me of a parakeet I had when I was young. I try to remember its name.

"Dan," the old man says. That was not the name of my parakeet.

"That's *my* name." My lover laughs, lifting toward me as much as he can. "He just said our names back-to-back. It's like our love planted them in his head!"

The tattooed man makes a puking noise.

For fun, I ask everyone to please mouth his name, just to see if the old man will say it next. I encourage them to hurry up and do it while the old man's head is flaccid beneath a layer of broth.

"Hector," whimpers the crying man.

"Sam," sings Elvis.

"Fuck you," says the tattooed man.

Dan and I watch the old man with anticipation. Finally his aged face surfaces, and he gums the taste of the broth droplets on his cheeks before saying "Lancelot."

"That proves it," my lover coos. "Our names before; it was magic." I nod and we project ourselves into each other's eyes.

I want this moment to stay. I want it to multiply on and on with the unnatural growth of things just before death, speeding off the pure fat of life's last seconds. I want the feeling of our brushing fingertips to breed like cancerous cells.

When the steel door opens, we all turn and stare. The old man sits up and blinks his wet lashes. A chef enters; his hands are busy sharpening a long knife against a stone. "Who first?" he barks. We're all silent, though I think I hear the old man whisper "Daisy."

"All right then." The chef points his knife at me and theatrically moves it around a little, like he's writing his name in the air. "Let's start with you, since you're the meatiest."

I turn to give my lover a farewell glance, but then his screams fill the room. "No!" he cries, thrashing madly and fishlike. "Take me in her place. Please, I'm begging you. Make her the very last one."

"Okay," agrees the chef. "Sure." But first he twirls his knife at me a little more, like he's casting a spell, just so I know who's in charge.

Two men wearing long oven gloves come over and cut my lover's ropes. Dan stretches his lips out to kiss me, but is too soon pulled away and carried from the room like a ladder—one man at his shoulders, one man at his feet. "Please," he shouts, "one kiss," but the two men aren't as permissive as the chef. His words don't register with them. They possibly do not speak English, or any language.

"That was a beautiful gesture," says the crying man. He's sobbing now. "Such love."

I figure Dan would want me to try to make the best of my borrowed time. I need a distraction from grief. "Do you sing?" I ask Elvis-Sam.

"Are you lonesome, tonight?" he croons. The garlic cloves really muffle his vibrato.

I'm about to request a happier song when the chef and his goons reenter. The tattooed man speaks up when he sees them.

"I'll go," he says, "I hate these people."

So they take him. As he's pulled from the water, we see that he also has a tattoo on his arm that reads, MOTHER. This makes Crying-Hector cry even harder. "I should've called my mother more," he laments. "Told her I love her and appreciate her sacrifices." He takes in a deep breath. "We actually smell a little like her cooking."

"This one's for Mother," says Elvis-Sam. He begins singing again. "Mama liked the roses . . ."

"I'm not imagining the Elvis thing, right?" I ask him. "Did you work as an impersonator?"

Crying-Hector's wails are uncontrollable. Ripples in the broth start moving from his torso over to mine. They're lapping at my stomach like a soft current.

His emotion touches me. I want to extend my foot across our little bullion pond and wipe his tears with my brothy toes, but my legs are bound together at the ankles.

When the door opens, four new henchmen, increasingly sour from the first to the fourth, enter with the chef. "I need two this time," he orders. The men grab Elvis-Sam and Crying-Hector, who continue singing and weeping respectively as they are carried away.

Alone with the old man it is very quiet, and I realize how loud the boiling noises have become. He lifts his head and says, "Heidi."

I knew a Heidi once. From ballet class in high school. I pause and imagine being taken from the kettle and laid onto a silver platter next to a ten-foot-tall layer cake, and on top of that cake is Heidi, tied and gagged and mounted in a pirouette pose. When she sees me, our eyes exchange wide glances of recognition and tender helplessness.

"Lacey," the old man says. As they pull him from the broth, I see he's missing a leg. I wonder if he arrived with it missing, or if they ate his leg and then put him back.

With the others all gone, the boiling bubbles feel far more scalding than before. I am bad at science and don't know if before we had all somehow shared the heat but now I alone bear its brunt. It seems so. I miss my lover, and this additional suffering perhaps makes the broth feel hotter as well.

As the footsteps come, I wonder if there will be anything after death. I try to think of Dan waiting for me on the other side, our budding love being allowed to blossom from the beyond. But my mind keeps trying to prepare for what it will feel like if they don't kill me before they start cutting me up. "There are worse ways to die," I tell myself, "than being boiled and then sliced with a knife." But it takes me a while to think of one.

I do, though, finally. I imagine being carried out the door to a table where all five of my kettle-mates are waiting, free and unbound, silverware in hand. Though they're dry and dressed now, their skins are still flushed from their time in the broth. I imagine Dan saying he has dibs on my heart, and the others laughing; Elvis-Sam singing "Love Me Tender," as my carving starts and I lose consciousness to the sounds of battling forks and knives. This daydream dampens the horror of my fate like a bowl placed over a candle. You can bear anything, I tell myself, if you know you're not alone, and the cold air stings my boiled skin as the chef's men lift me into their arms. Their grip has the strength of apathy, and this is a comfort; I'm only going where the others have already been.

Model's Assistant

My best friend, Garla, is a model from somewhere Swedishy; when people try to pin down where she just yells, "Vodka," or if she's in a better mood, "Vodka, you know?" which seems like she's maybe saying she's Russian, but really she just wants to drink. Wherever she's from, Garla now lives inside the bubble of model-land. I wish I lived in model-land, too, but the closest I can come is hanging out with Garla, which is like going on vacation to a model-land time-share.

We met at a party in Chelsea that I pond-skipped to. I definitely wasn't invited. I'd gone with a real friend to a not-so-hot party, and then left with her friend to go to a better party where I met a stranger who took me to a quite hot party. It was there that I made out with the photographer who took me to the party of Garla. She wasn't hosting it but she was present, and anywhere Garla goes is Garla's party.

I think the only reason I ever saw Garla again was because I was drunk enough to tell her the truth. She was trying on bizarre clothes—there was a shroud that looked space-like yet medical, like a gown one might wear to get a pap smear on Mars. Then she put on a dress whose pleating created the suggestion of a displaced goiter somewhere to the left of her neck and she sashayed toward me. I was holding my head onto my body, carefully and by the window, so that its breeze might sober me up enough to walk to the end of the room, where I might then become sober enough to walk to the toilet and land on the floor. There, hopefully, the pressure from my cheek against my cell phone could call someone who knew me and liked me enough to get me a cab and make sure this night was not where my life's journey would end. But for all I knew it was, and when I saw Garla I held on to my head just a little bit tighter, because she appeared to be strutting over to rip it off.

"You," she said, and I straightened up grammar-school style. I puked in my mouth but absolutely did not open my lips and let it fall on the floor. "Do you like this?" She did a turn that looked so elegant and stylized and unteachable to everyone in the room but to Garla was just something that accidentally slipped out of her like a tiny fart.

"It makes you look like you're pregnant in the back," I said, using the nose of my beer bottle to itch between my shoulder blades, where the seam of her dress inexplicably globed out. She scowled and pranced off. I assumed she was offended until she brought over a silver-plated bowl filled with the car keys of various guests.

"Use for vomit," she said, and then, "have phone," and slipped a crystal-encrusted device into my purse. I think at that point two large gray wolfhounds magically walked up to either side of her and the three of them then headed toward the kitchen. "You love dogs and have a tendency to hallucinate them," I told myself as I stumbled toward the bathroom. Various refined guests stared on in horror as I groped onto pieces of furniture and potted plants, trying to stabilize my journey into a small room housing cold linoleum and a sink. "Why am I always the nerd at the party?" I thought. "I am in my thirties and by now I should at least know how to pretend."

The thing about bathrooms in parties is they don't always stay bathrooms; they start out as such but then become make-out rooms or cocaine-snorting rooms or bubble-bath-orgy rooms. When I burst through the door holding my abdomen, a slight and waify couple seemed to be using it as a now-that-we've-agreed-the-night-will-end-with-mutual-oral-sex-let's-take-our-time-getting-buzzed-first room; they were drinking very red wine, sitting on the side of the bathtub and giggling, using fingertips of wine to draw simple pictures onto the shower's white tile. The "braap" sound I made while becoming sick intrigued them. They were in their early twenties, and I could feel them looking at me with something real and concentrated. I don't think it was pity as much as curiosity; they seemed to wonder very much what it might be like to be so uncomposed. "I don't get when people use puking in art," said the boy, and the girl said, "Well, it's not like that, when they do," meaning not like me but like Garla throwing up pink paint onto a teal ceramic raccoon.

"I need a cab," I mumbled, and the boy was sympathetic but firm. "I won't touch you," he said.

"No," I agreed. "I'll get myself down to the door."

It took a great while to do this. At some point I wondered if I should try to find Garla and give her the phone back, but then I saw a burst of light across the living room and there she was, the camera's flash bouncing off her oiled thigh, her foot inside the host's tropical aquarium. Everyone wanted a shot of her leather bondage shoe surrounded by fake coral: people were holding up cell phones and professional equipment and thin digital cameras; "Tickle fish," Garla was saying to everyone, which continually prompted a laugh-track response from the entire crowd. There was no way I could deal with calling her name and having that amount of attention suddenly focus over to my own body. Plus I didn't really want to give it back. A supermodel's phone! I was like a turd inside someone who'd accidentally swallowed an engagement ring: though I was nothing myself, I now carried something uniquely special.

I fell easily down the stairs and by the time I was able to stand, to my great surprise, a cab had come. "Thank you," I called up to the couple in the bathroom, but it came out gurgled, and they were likely busy readying to use their youth and beauty to give one another endless reciprocal orgasms.

I kept the phone on my desk for several days wondering what to do about it. There was something wrong with the phone; it didn't ring. Garla's phone would ring, wouldn't it?

It didn't ring until the fourth day.

"Hi, Womun." It was Garla. I began explaining how I'd meant to give the phone back, how I certainly hadn't called various pawnshops to price it (had!), but she interrupted. "It your phone, for me. I call you with it," she said, to which I could've said a lot of things, like how I already have a phone, or that I was very afraid of getting killed for this jewel-phone, should someone see me talking on it in my neighborhood, because I don't have a lot of money and neither does anyone else who lives here, but oftentimes people badly need money, and desperate times/desperate measures.

"I get you for fashion show," she said, "tonight at the seven-thirty." Out of some type of pride I wanted to make sure she didn't mean that *I* would be in the fashion show, that it wasn't an ironic thing where Beautifuls each try to snag themselves an Ugly, and whoever snags the ugliest Ugly and dresses it up best is the winner. "You mean go watch one with you?" I asked, and she said, "Ha," then it sounded like she lit a cigarette or something and said, "Ha. Ha. I mean this," and told me where to meet her.

Since that night my life has changed in many ways. I'm still no one, unless I am with Garla, and then I become *with Garla*, a new, exciting identity that makes nearly everything possible, except being attractive myself. And except being important when I am not with Garla.

At the oxygen bar, Garla gives my face three firm slaps on the cheek. She is always taking grandmotherly liberties such as these. "Put you in special coffin," she says, which is a term of endearment on her part but I don't know what it means exactly. I like to think that it's a sort of Snow White reference, that I'm so dear to her that she wants to keep my body displayed in a glass box next to her couch, forever asleep. Though I guess it could also mean she wants to close me inside an iron maiden.

Garla is sitting in front of a laptop with a solar charger plugged into it, although it is raining outside and we are in a darkened room. Garla doesn't have opinions on things; she's not really the pro or con type. Right now she is into being very anti-global warming because she knows that being very anti–global warming is chic. Either things are chic or they aren't, and if they're chic then they're for Garla. "The web won't come," Garla says.

"Solar charger," I point out. "No sun."

"Global warming," Garla says. She will often randomly say the media titles of topics and events, such as "Crisis in Darfur," then take a drink and be silent for a few more hours.

A waitress wearing a hemp robe enters with two tanks and two breathing masks, hooking Garla in first. With the mask on Garla appears to be a pilot from the future, possibly a computer-generated one. Her perfect skin looks like a plasma screen.

"Are you from Sweden?" the waitress asks.

"Vodka, you know?" says Garla, and the waitress's eyes frown; perhaps she has just Botoxed because I can tell she wants to make an expression but instead she blinks a few times.

"Could she get a glass of vodka," I ask, and the woman mentions that alcohol is not usually consumed during the treatment. She is already on the way to get it, though, and when she returns there's also a glass for me.

It gets a little overwhelming in the mask when the pure oxygen starts to hit us at the same time as the vodka. Garla takes my hand. I don't know if I'm attracted to her or if she's just beautiful. I think it's the latter because she doesn't say much, and what she does say doesn't make much sense to me. But people don't have to talk a lot or make sense for others to love them. Just look at dogs and babies.

"Cloud of vodka!" Garla screams. I decide she wants another glass because I want another glass, so I hold two fingers up at the woman in hemp while pointing down to our melted ice. My fingers stay in an upright "peace" position; with our masks I imagine that Garla and I are on some kind of extreme roller coaster that goes into the stratosphere, and we're passing the camera that takes a picture for us to buy at the end, and I am saying, "This is me and Garla. Peace."

She has made me the best-dressed party nerd of all time. Once, she put these chain-link pants on me and I couldn't move, not even like a robot. So Garla—wearing six-inch stiletto heels—actually picked me up, carried me up the stairs to the party, and planted me by yet another fish tank, either so I'd have something to watch or because she knew that at some point, a part of her body would be posing inside of it and she very much wanted for me to be there to say, "Now Garla has to go home" when it started to get boring for her.

There was never a conversation where Garla hired me to be her assistant. I just started speaking up when it made sense to, like when a director asked if he could film himself cutting her arm a tiny bit with a designer katana sword and licking her blood off the blade, and she answered him with "Special coffin," in a very small voice. "We have to go, Garla," I used to say, but I soon learned that "Garla has to go" is a better way to phrase it, because then it seems like she doesn't have a choice.

Tonight we go to another fashion show. Garla's walking in it so I wait backstage in the chair where her makeup was done, and at several points people inquire as to why I'm there. Very few actually want me to leave; they're just baffled.

Afterward we go to the home of a fellow model where I watch Garla drink herself into a deep sea. She is a metronomic drinker. I can count the glasses she drinks per hour, like a time signature, and know exactly how drunk she is at any given moment. With me it's the opposite; the drunk is that mystery wedding guest who may show up early, late, or not at all.

By four A.M. Garla is lying on an island countertop in the kitchen. Some guy has dumped a miniature Buddhist sand garden out on her abdomen, and he's swirling the sand around her belly button with a tiny bamboo rake. Her head is hanging off the counter; it's flipped back like a Pez dispenser, and I walk over and we have this intoxicated moment.

"I know you're more," my drunken eyes say. They say this in a breathy, hesitant manner that insists it has taken a lot of time for them to work up the courage to say such a thing, without words nonetheless.

"Yes," answer Garla's eyes, and like all of Garla's answers it is a mysterious pearl whose full value I begin to appraise immediately. I walk over to her and lift her head up with my hands so it is level with the counter, holding it. I look down at her like a surgeon.

"Some type of sausage," Garla says; she likes the cured meats.

For a second I have the urge to drop her head. I'm reminded of being a child on the beach, the shells I'd leap to pick up and then throw back. They always seemed of greater worth from a distance, beneath the water.

I keep wondering if Garla will ask me to quit my job copyediting and join her full-time in model-land. Her agency is very good to her, but I know she needs me, or at least could really use me, more than she does, which leads me to wonder two things: Does Garla have others like Me? If so, how many Mes are there? Does she really need Me at all? The thing about Garla is that it's always okay for Garla. No matter what happens, Garla will be okay. I just speed the okayness up a little bit for her so that okay is sure to happen in real time.

Although my life has many more great things in it now than before I met Garla, I'm still beginning to feel a bit used.

And—how can I deny this—I want more of Garla. She is a rare substance, if only because of the role and power she has in our society and not anything she holds innately. Rare substances make people feel selfish and greedy, and Garla is no exception. Neither am I.

I am also getting a little sick of my special Garla-phone, but it's really expensive and the only thing Garla will call me on. I got rid of my other phone and now have only the phone Garla gave me, perhaps because I know she intended it to only be used when she called me, and this is a small rebellion on my part. Garla doesn't pick up on rebellions, though, big or small. She has no need for them.

I decide to ask if I can be her paid assistant, because she probably will not say yes or no, and I can just interpret it as yes. If anything, by quitting my job and hanging out with her more I will get additional goodies I can sell online, and Garla's schwag pays several times more than my current employer.

I strike when we are in the back of a town car on the way to a designer's private shoot. Garla is stretched out on my lap with her muss of blond hair hanging down over my knees. Her hair is softer than my shaved legs.

"Garla," I say, "I'm going to quit my job and be your assistant. You don't have to pay me hardly anything. I don't make very much as it is." There's a pause and she hands up a tiny golden comb to me, I presume for me to begin brushing her hair with. I also presume this means "yes," is a quid pro quo gesture. I call my boss right then on the Garla-phone and quit as loudly as I can without seeming hostile, just to try to burn the event a little deeper into the ether of Garla's memory.

The shoot goes well. Afterward I take her glasses of chilled vodka that look like refreshing water and we have a look at the pictures, which are beautiful. We leave with giant bags of expensive clothing that we neither paid nor asked for.

I am feeling more visible by the second. Perhaps, I think, I should move into Garla's apartment. That way I'd always be right there to meet her needs and there wouldn't be all the Garla-phone calls in the middle of the night; she could just yell or do a special grunt. Though I've never heard Garla yell. Everyone is already paying attention.

Except the next morning, she doesn't answer my calls, and she doesn't call me. This goes on for a week and a half. I sulk like a real model. I don't eat and I drink lots of vodka and I cut my own hair in the bathroom with dull scissors and then regret it, and the next morning I think about going to a really expensive salon and having it fixed except I don't have the money for that, especially now that I have no job. For that, I need Garla.

This is the root of my pain. I had convinced myself that she needed me, specifically, when really, anyone could and would do what I did: follow around a gorgeous person and get gifts and call outrages by name for what they are. How did I lend any type of panache to that role? Looking in the mirror at my botched home haircut, I realize that my new expensive clothes still look nerdy because they don't fit me right. They never will.

When the Garla-phone finally lights up and makes its synthetic music, it's like an air-raid siren. I'm paralyzed with fear but angst-ridden from loneliness and desperation. "Where have you been?" I scream. "We agreed I'd be your assistant. I quit my job! I haven't seen you for like ten days!"

"Vodka head," Garla explains.

I want to pretend like nothing is wrong. "I'm not a bad

assistant," I say. "I'm a good assistant, which means I need to be where you are, and help you with things."

"Later, a party," she says. I can hear happy screams in the background and their shrillness stabs into me. I know those screams belong to completely impractical people, and I hate that she chose them over me. "What time?" I ask, but she already hung up.

Eventually she does text me the party's address. I stop by a nearby bar to have a few drinks alone first. It feels good to sulk over a glass in public. How could I have let my guard down so badly? Before Garla, I had been all-guard. Before Garla, I would've seen Garla coming. My pre-Garla life suddenly seems like an amazing thing; I hadn't even known what I was missing. As I walk out of the bar and look up near the balcony I'm headed to, I can actually see Garla. It makes me feel creepy but I stand there and watch for a while anyway, until the two of us seem like strangers. Even at this distance and with the party's disco lights, it's clear she has dazzling bone structure.

Compared to her, I am like a sandwich. I am completely inhuman and benign. I try to remember a sandwich I ate in the fourth grade and cannot. I can't even really remember one I ate a month ago. We all must be like fourth-grade sandwiches to Garla.

It's not until I get inside the suite and look around that I realize it's the same residence where Garla and I first met. This makes my hands and feet sweat rapidly; the line is becoming a circle.

As the night moves on, it's like going back in time. When I enter, Garla gives me a soft embrace and kisses my cheek, but I want restitution. I quit my job and had the week from hell, and she isn't going to reenter my life with one quick, pouty smile. Maybe I'm replaceable, but I don't have to be happy about it.

I take my old seat by the window and start rapidly boozing. The lights change colors in ways that suggest I'm going too fast, and that is the speed I want to go. It's a rush, like skydiving. I keep giving Garla a scowl that says, "Hey, you. I'm not holding on. I'm in free fall."

She's rubbing pieces of chocolate over her lips like ChapStick and men are helplessly pulled to her side of the room. Garla's face is a centrifuge that separates the confident from the weak and the jealous, and I have been spun away.

Stumbling to the bathroom, I get out my jeweled Garla-phone. Part of me wants to put it into the toilet, or at least try to see if it will fit through the hole in the bottom of the bowl. I want to throw up on it but it is so shiny that with its sparkling crystals and my drunken compound fly-eye vision, I have no aim. Instead the puke falls into the water and the phone falls on the ground, and when I'm finished and my cheek hits the floor the phone looks like a store of riches behind the plunger. I grab the phone and open it, kind of bumping it around, hoping it will call a friend who will come pick me up.

But it's Garla's phone, so it calls Garla. I hang up but a few minutes later she's standing over me in an Amazonian manner, one leg on either side of my body. "Put you in tiny coffin," she says, rolling out some toilet paper and batting it against my wet cheek.

"I wish you would."

She doesn't appreciate my display of self-pity. I watch her toss her martini glass out the window onto the patio, where it breaks. "You go home and rest doctor-television."

After she leaves, a bodyguard enters and picks me up with a disgusted look, like he's emptying a full bedpan. He helps me into the taxi. Motoring away, I watch the colored streaks of Garla on the patio upstairs.

In a panic I check my purse to make sure I still have it: the Garla-phone, the jewel. The cursed treasure that brought distress alongside fortune. Glistening in my lap, it is too beautiful to be trusted. The cab nears my apartment, and I have the urge to leave the phone behind on the seat for someone else to find and answer. But I won't. Instead I'll go home and wait for her to call me and turn me into something special for however long she wants, and this time I won't forget to be grateful.

Porn Star

I'm expected to have anal sex with the winning contestant on the moon. I work on an Adult Network reality show called *Eat It*, where male contestants eat all they can of a given substance in order to win some level of fornication with the program's hostesses. Our show's executives decided to do a space episode for the season finale to beat the competition in terms of filming in extreme, sensational locations.

I found out that I got the space bid at a surprise luncheon in my honor. They gave me champagne and several helium-filled balloons with silver moons on the sides. I began to recall a documentary on the Discovery Channel about bathrooms on spaceships. Apparently the toilet sucks it in. It is like a pee-vacuum.

"Space itself is one big vacuum," said Dick, the show's host. He handed me a cupcake decorated with a frosting rocket ship. Dick is responsible for overseeing the eating contests and judging the line between an acceptable gag and a disqualifying vomit.

Throughout the party I smiled at the bad puns, the jokes about "reentry." As I left, my coworker Priscilla told me how lucky I was.

"Space is like . . . hot right now, you know? An exclusive club."

That night after a shower I stared down at my nipples and their bumpy, vaguely lunar surface. I checked the show's online message boards to see what people were saying about my selection. Even though I've only been on the show for one season, I'm a hit with viewers.

GoodEatFan from New Jersey wrote, *Her breasts have a soft expanding look about them, like rising bread.* Most of them talk about my trademark—my hair. It's really brown and thick and long, and every contestant I've ever been assigned to, before we start doing anything, has always turned me around and pushed his member into my hair. It's the first thing that happens, every time. Of course that won't be possible on the moon.

Before I even meet the contestants, the show execs and I watch them get interviewed. We spy in on their conversation through a one-way mirror, giving the whole situation a police-sting kind of feel.

The contestants I'll be doing the show with are Guff, Leo, and Bill. Guff owns his own fertilizer company and is by far the largest of the bunch. His voice is crazy-deep. Dick can't get over it.

"If James Earl Jones yodeled into the universe's vagina, Guff's voice is the noise that would echo back."

Kevin in HR agrees. "His chest seems supported by some exterior plate that's masked with hair."

A hidden camera—they're everywhere—zooms in on Guff's face. He is a mouth-breather. His teeth are a variety of sizes in all the wrong places, as if they'd once fallen out and he had to shove them back in a hurry with no regard to their original position. He looks naked without a log of wood beneath his arm, though this is the first time I've ever seen him, and he's logless. I bet he likes waffles.

Leo is physically much smaller than I am. What's sad is, I can tell he thinks he really dressed up for the audition. His shirt is buttoned all the way up and the way his hair is wet-combed and parted reminds me of an antique ventriloquist's dummy. The executives mumble that he doesn't look healthy, and they're right. Something's off. When I glance at Leo, it's like seeing a lemon the color of tooth enamel.

Sheila, the only other female in the room, says, "It's as if he lives in a median between our world and a planet of anemic man-lizards. He lives there in his car." Sheila's an exec, not a do-er, but she seems to constantly place herself in do-er shoes and ask, Who could ever touch him? She's asking this question to everyone but me. I'm the answer, though, so I speak up.

"I vote keep him. He won't be any trouble. It's more than we can say about Guff."

A consenting murmur makes its way around the table.

Bill is Bill. Each episode they choose at least one contestant who could be misconstrued, on a good day, as not completely repulsive, and this episode it's Bill. The fact that he knows this, that he's receiving "hottie billing," makes him so much more sleazy and disgusting than the others. He is in no way actually attractive. Instead of "for sure," he keeps saying, "for surely." The interviewer finally asks if Shirley is someone close to him. He roars. He acts as if he's met his comical match and tries to give a high five, which the interviewer does not take him up on.

⬛⬛⬛⬛

I meet the contestants in person on the first day of physical training. It's being taped as bonus footage for the season's DVD. We're going to put on the space suits and walk around in an underwater tank.

Guff, who apparently developed extraordinary lung capacity by playing the baritone through high school, is requesting he not have to wear the suit or receive oxygen.

"I've got heavy boots," he says. "I'll just walk with you on the bottom."

"No showing off," I tease. I'm supposed to tease. I'm wearing a surfer-style bodysuit that has breast-like gel inserts sewn into the chest pockets. My actual breasts are spilling out the top of the suit, creating the effect that they're jewels of a much larger crown. Occasionally I remember that I'm the lone woman on the entire set and that everyone is staring at me, but it's something that only comes back to me every twenty minutes or so, about five minutes after I recall that I'm completely stoned.

"Your beauty is beautiful," Guff says, then immediately realizes redundancy. Before he starts trying to dig himself out of that hole, I notice he's eating a package of Lance Peanut Butter Crackers.

"Are those things ever fresh?" I ask.

He looks down at the package as though it will give him the answer. Neon-orange crumbs are furrowed in his beard like lice from another planet.

"I just mean," I say, "every time I see them in a vending machine, they look like they've been sitting there since the seventies. Maybe it's the wrappers."

Guff's chest starts heaving up and down, and I take a few steps back. It's possible that Lance products from vending machines are the only thing he ever eats and that they are the source of his superhuman size and strength. Maybe before he found Lance products he was as thin as Leo. I suddenly worry that I just insulted his favorite thing in life. I think about how I would feel if someone came up to me and said, "What are Valium addicts thinking? Pills can never make you truly happy!"

But instead he starts laughing, guttural undulations somewhere between the Green Giant and Santa. Leo walks over to the corner of the room, curling to it like it's his mother. He whispers, "I love those crackers."

Guff likes this. It doesn't take long before brains meet brawn and the two of them form a symbiotic relationship, like barnacle and whale. When they stand next to each other, I get the feeling that Leo recently broke out of Guff's chest, that he started as a tapeworm but fought his way up the evolutionary ladder.

Bill, of course, is too good to talk to anyone but me. I notice that his enormous gold watch doesn't work.

A medical crew puts us through a series of tests to check our vitals: treadmill running, push-ups, that sort of thing. Bill keeps checking out his own ass in the mirror. I watch him stare at my ass, then his ass, then mine, then his, as though they're having a conversation with one another and only he can hear it.

Leo has taken this occasion as an opportunity to quit smoking, which is laudable, except the combination of physical exertion and nicotine patches is making him ill. When it's his turn for the treadmill, he runs over and his shirt is soaked from warm-ups. He peels it off and there are already four patches over his chest, sitting almost exactly where the doctor intends to put the electrodes.

"Are those patches supposed to be placed directly over the heart?" I ask. A former contestant I had to sleep with wore a patch once. When he said to me, Baby, watch the patch, eh?, I first stared with confusion at his small, triangular goatee. But then he lifted his sleeve and displayed the patch with great pride, the way a fifth grader might show off a temporary tattoo of a cobra. Apparently it hurts if the patches get bumped, which he used as an excuse to not flex his arms for me. As if I'd been looking forward to that.

We wait until Leo is done throwing up and then go get into our suits. Once inside, Leo's arms, which previously looked like blanched string beans, now appear to be relatively the same size as Bill's. This boosts his confidence.

Guff and Leo solidify their union underwater. Instead of using the reach-claw we've been provided with, Guff places Leo on his shoulders and operates him like an extended limb. Bill keeps dropping his claw and cursing into his headset microphone. He is unable to complete his "mission" of using the claw to tighten a loose bolt.

I take a moment and enjoy the secluded world we've entered, in addition to my new role as an asexual giant. It's fun to be individually wrapped and surrounded by water on all sides. Just when I'm starting to feel like one of the guys, Bill lumbers over.

"Wanna see my electric eel?"

He places his fishbowl head against mine, and we clink like crystal glasses toasting.

At lunch Guff, like some steroidal Oliver Twist from the lumber-and-fur orphanage, devours all the complimentary sandwiches and then asks for more. Leo ended up having to eat activated charcoal. When we were coming up from the water he puked in his suit, specifically inside his face helmet. It covered the entire lens and made it impossible to tell whether he'd gotten sick or his head had exploded. Bill claimed to have lost his appetite over this incident, but after desuiting I saw him help himself to a shrimp cocktail.

The rest of the day it's just Guff, Bill, and me. Leo has taken the afternoon off to recover. Guff keeps giving Bill this odd look out the corner of his eye, like he knows Bill is hiding a cookie in one of his pockets—he just can't figure out which one.

There's little discussion about what I'm going up to the moon to do. I wonder what their advertising spin is going to be; if they're planning on billing me as space's first whore. I try not to let those types of words bother me. At least I'm not giving people root canals. At least I'm not putting makeup on the dead.

As the day ends, the show's executives give us a sneak peak at our real suits. By us, I mean whoever wins and myself. Each suit has a small portal; mine's in the back and his is in the front. The man who's explaining it to us connects the portals to one another, like marching elephants clinging trunks to tails. Once they're aligned, they open, pressurize, and retract to an acceptable length. This way he can enter me. On the moon.

Because I'll be in a suit and will look like a hulking male physicist from behind, they've outfitted the back of my helmet with a monitor. It'll show footage of me, doing what we'll be doing, only un-space-suited.

"Any questions?" the scientist asks.

Bill has one. "Can you like, kneel down and stuff?"

I imagine Bill's panting coming through my headset in stereo. It's going to sound like he's in boot camp fulfilling a midday order to dig a ten-foot latrine. The secret to having sex with people who make disgusting sounds is to out-moan them. It gets them there quicker, too, which is half the battle.

A few days before the launch, the contestants are brought in to sample the eat-off product, which was partially designed by NASA. We can't use any foods that could break off and create airborne crumbs, so the execs chose a type of hybrid sausage. It's a gelatinous, partial-meat substance that won't flake or fragment.

"Could we make this peanut butterier?" Guff's vote for a flavor infusion is denied.

"It doesn't smell like anything," says Leo. This is true, but Leo says this carefully, as if he knows they're about to tell him, It smells delicious.

"Actually," says one scientist, "it should smell like plastic."

Leo sniffs again. He nods.

Bill is holding a coil of sausage in two fingers, like it's the world's longest cigar.

"Uh," says Bill.

This should be good.

"I mean, do we have to eat something that looks so much like a you-know-what? Once in a while people even say the word 'sausage' instead of saying you-know-what."

"It's just food," I tell him. "It's just meat."

"Well," says the scientist, "it's not *just* meat." He lists off several ingredients not found in either sausages or you-know-whats.

We're told the eat-off contest will take place when the ship is hovering over the moon. The winning contestant and I will then travel in a small capsule to the lunar surface to perform the sex act. The way the executive describes it sounds oddly like a honeymoon, a man and wife being escorted off to more private quarters post-ceremony.

Blastoff is hard. There's a moment when my mind tells me that we've blown up, and it takes a few more seconds to realize that we haven't. It feels like gravity wants to separate my skeleton from my flesh.

Then everything stops. The cabin is instantly too still. When I look at my reflection in a chrome panel, the expression on my face seems a thousand years old.

Bill mutters something about being a space cowboy. I'm staring at Dick, the only one here I really know. He's looking out the window, and he seems horrified. Instead of coming with me and the contestants to train before the launch, he opted to prepare using his own regimen of hypnosis and magnet therapy.

"Dick, are you okay?" My voice sounds weird. I decide I should just have a space persona, different even from my porn persona, and that way I can quit feeling so uncomfortable about nothing being the same. I secretly rename myself Zero G and bat my eyelashes at the lack of gravity.

But Dick is not okay.

He's a big tanning bed fan, which perhaps explains his sudden preoccupation with the sun.

"Where is the sun?" He keeps screaming this. It's making Leo unsettled. Guff is looking for the sun inside the cabin.

Bill is trying to recite a list of one-liners from memory and keeps having to look down at the cheat sheet in his hand. Most of the hottie-billing contestants try to memorize jokes before taping. But once the camera starts rolling, they never remember them. Never.

━━━━━━

The medical adviser/cameraman tranquilizes Dick and straps him into a cocoon-bed on the wall. It looks as though some giant spider caught him and hung him there. I keep watching the cargo door for a human-sized space arachnid to enter and devour him whole. I rub Dick's arm a little bit and drool comes out of his mouth. It's decided that I'll host the show on my own.

We take about an hour or so to tumble through the air and get used to weightlessness. Quarters are tight and Bill keeps reaching out to tickle my feet. I can feel my stomach and my crotch in the same place; there is no middle. Just my head and then everything else.

"I really don't feel like eating," Leo says as they give him his food-coil. After several debates, the execs decided to wrap it in yet another layer of edible protective casing. If the coil were actually dropped onto the ground on Earth, it would probably bounce.

Bill points to my chest for the camera. "I've got all the inspiration I need right there," he says. I want to remind Bill that even if he wins, he won't be seeing or touching my breasts at any point in time. But I don't. I get out my stopwatch for the eat-off. Guff has already opened his mouth wide in a head start.

"Ready . . . get set . . . go!"

The first thirty seconds of the race are always the best, showcasing an initial rush of adrenaline. For a moment, it seems like anyone's game. Guff starts too quickly, devouring the first two feet of sausage for a huge lead before coming to a standstill.

Bill is hurting; it's clear. I know a lot about the gag reflex. Throats are usually one-way lanes, up or down, and it's my professional opinion that Bill's throat is about to switch to rising motion.

Leo, skinny dark-horse candidate Leo, is surprising us all. He's eating in snakelike motions, slithering his coil down like it's one of his own organs that he coughed up on accident—there's a place for it, and he knows where it goes, and he's putting it there.

In the last thirty seconds, Bill has to quit and strap on his sick bag. It Velcros to his face like a giant gray shoe. I watch with pleasure as his abdominal contortions propel him around the cabin.

Guff slows to near-stillness like a gargantuan spent windup toy. Leo finishes ten seconds before the deadline. We declare him the winner, and as he and I get strapped into the craft that will take us down to the moon's surface, he keeps saying, "I've never won anything before."

As we step out I feel like there's a tree growing inside my ribs whose leaves weigh fifty pounds each. They keep falling off and floating down to my knees with a heavy thickness.

I'm watching Leo attempt a bouncing sort of walk when the intercom on my helmet beeps. "We're ready." It's one of the show's executives on Earth; I can't remember his name but he always wears funny ties. Funny in a bad way. Tiny cans of beer with angel wings.

Something about hearing his voice amidst all the nothingness makes me realize I'm being watched. It's a sensation that oddly has never occurred before in the past during any close-up, or even times when I had to squat over a toilet bowl that wasn't a bowl at all but a giant camera. I feel my fake-smile muscles involuntarily flex.

Leo gets behind me, and I give him an encouraging low-gravity pat on the arm. It takes a few moments for our suits' portals to align. When they open, it sounds like something very important is leaking out. The noise is high-pitched and quick, like wind from the future.

"Um . . . just a second," says Leo.

I tell him, "No rush; there isn't a time limit," although we're breathing tanked oxygen and there certainly is. When he finally enters me, I'm staring at Earth, which looks like the circular door of some ancient tomb, like if we could just reach out and slide it aside, we'd see the answer to something very important.

There's a hiccup of static and I can hear the execs talking: Why does this look so educational? and Should've gone with the body bubble. I moan their voices out.

"Er . . . just a sec," Leo says again.

"Take your time," I say, but I break from my sex-voice to say it. "Keep it hot," the intercom reminds me.

I feel fine but also very strange, looking at the world and its distance. I feel its weight in my stomach like a pregnancy, like an old meal. When I want to, I cover up the Earth and its oceans with my hand, and even with the cameras it seems like no one can see me.

Zookeeper

I took a baby panda home from the zoo. Technically, I was not supposed to. I decided to keep my job there, at least for a while, to avoid looking suspicious.

Dolores from reptiles almost got me.

"Aren't those panda droppings?" she asked, pointing to my hair.

"I don't think so," I said. I put on a helmet. The panda and I were still working through bathroom and sleeping arrangements.

I named her Lulu. Pandas really like bamboo. That's not a myth.

At the time I was living in a room of the Sleep-Eeze Inn. All my local calls were free, as was my cable. I put up a DO NOT DISTURB! sign but worried it might fall off, so I taped several others like it to the actual door.

One night I came home from work with some chicken tenders. I figured the two of us could share them. I did not bring enough for all the policemen who were outside my door.

I pretended to be part of the crowd. I pinched a mother of five on her elbow.

"What's up?" I asked.

She covered the ears of her youngest. "They thought someone was making a pornographic film in that room. There were all these signs up and people heard growling and scratching."

I saw them carrying out Lulu. She looked at me with her giant panda eyes.

"Mother," she yelled.

I didn't know that pandas could talk. It might have been an accident.

While the cops questioned me, Lulu and I tidied up what was left of the continental breakfast in the lounge. I stuck Froot Loops on the tips of her canine teeth. She seemed to be smiling.

I went to jail. Lulu went to the zoo.

There's a website, freelulu.com, that has a photo of both of us standing behind our respective bars.

Each month I write the zoo a letter, in cursive, asking them to send me a lock of her hair. They will not. People ask why I did it, which is hard to explain. I usually tell them, "She was soft."

Bandleader's Girlfriend

"You are embarrassing yourself on a national level," Sister yells into the phone. "What about Dead Mom?"

Dead Mom is not a mellow subject. I look over at my dearest lover, CT, who is lying on the couch rubbing slices of ripe grape-fruit across his chest. He's watching a television program about sexual behavior in dolphins.

"Such liquid-rubber bodies," he whispers. CT is the lead singer for Wolf Rainbow. They are a total hit but CT doesn't measure success in terms of money; true success lies in Worm Vibrations, or wormbrations.

"CT" stands for "Coppertone." He is into the rays of the sun.

Sister clears her throat. Talking with her makes me feel a little cosmically disturbed. I try to remind myself that she has invested a lot of time in me, that it became quite a habit for her, a *passion,* even, and I think it is important for people to follow their passion. Unless, like Sister's, they hinder another's enlightenment. Namely mine.

My enlightenment is sparkling pink water and Sister is a levee, but CT allows me to rise up and overwhelm her walls. Sister has never before experienced the unrestricted passion of one as enlightened to the Worm as CT is. She has no idea what to do with such emotion.

A good example of this occurred when I took CT home for Thanksgiving and Sis extended her hand to him.

"Mother of my love-cub, I greet you," he said, and softly licked her face. After this display of vulnerability Sis's vibes were very tight and secluded. The corners of her mouth tucked themselves in firmly like hotel bedsheets.

CT and I prefer to sleep outdoors but sometimes we're forced to stay in really nice hotels. It's all Management. If it were up to CT we'd just find a field close to our next venue and sleep there, but Management makes some good points: privacy, etc. CT's nightly rituals, which are not exclusionary of nudity and spiritual vision accelerators for communication with the Worm Eternal, can be wrongly interpreted by people like the authorities.

Grog, Wolf Rainbow's bassist, uses humor to mask his negative thinking when he agrees with Management about hotels. He says things like "How can I round up babes for bonefests and take them to the middle of a cornfield? The hottest babes with the biggest milkbags will not go for this. They want open bars and heart-shaped beds. Such are the desires of those with giant milkbags." Then he'll pause, adding, "I can't believe you sleep in the buff where it is wild and shit. What if a snake bit your johnson?"

Now Sister gives a loud gasp. She always talks so quickly that what she says seems urgent and true. It is some kind of trick. "You're on nearly every television station right now! I called because I need to talk to you about something serious, and now there's this drama. Do you ever stop to think about how your actions affect others? I mean what if deceased loved ones get *one* day to peek down to Earth from Heaven and Tuesday was the *one* day Mom had for all eternity to check up on us and our lives? When she opened the clouds she would've been greeted with your . . . your spectacle." Sister begins crying.

I know from experience that her tears aren't clear; they're a strange gray color like weird steam. I always figured they were mixing with her gothish makeup until I realized she doesn't wear any. Her face is just kind of gray, too, because she never goes outside; she fears nature like it's a rapist or murderer, even though, as I tell her all the time, it's *so* the opposite—*nature* is what's getting raped and murdered! But despite not having sun damage she got wrinkles before her time from watching constant news television and subconsciously reproducing the expressions of worry-stricken anchors.

Sister likes to pull back the curtains of her windows, then stare out of them and look up at the sky suspiciously.

"What did you want to talk about?" I ask. "Do you need some money?" Of late, Sister has been plagued with a variety of fiscal obligations. "Listen, Sis, I do understand what you're saying." I peek behind my shoulder and watch CT—naked, gentle CT, pink grapefruit juices dripping down his body like cartoon sweat— pretend to plug the blowhole of the dolphin on television with a slice of his grapefruit. His giggles are like heartbeats: steady and seconds apart. "But you just have to realize that we're on different planes of existence. I'm not saying I'm better than you, just that my path is way more open with lots more colors."

Sister's weeping intensifies. "What the hell are you talking about?" she asks. "You're speaking the drug-talk. I want Claudia back."

If the spasm that afflicts my back and spine at the mention of the name "Claudia" could make a sound, a single note, it would be unharmonious beyond this dimension. Such a wonky note that no one would even be able to hear it, because evolution's design protects us. It's one of those things; the sound is made but does anyone hear it? Was it made? I speak but Sister does not hear me. Do I speak?

"Uuuuuuuhhhhhhhhhmmnnnngg." CT lets out a guttural moan to begin his A.M. bowel gyrations. His torso bounces up and down while his hips move like he's using an invisible Hula-Hoop.

His is a Hula-Hoop made of enchantment. It's built of understanding, spiritual experience, and opium ether, in addition to a variety of invisible delights. Most of our senses are completely inadequate and not to be trusted; our true feelings come from our wormholes, often described as "the heart in our stomach between our legs."

"Think about it," CT likes to say, "the organ that the wormless refer to as 'heart' is like, entirely muscle. A bodybuilder. A worker bee. Do bees have muscles?"

Sister does not affect my wormhole, but her disapproval makes my pulse quite irregular.

"Sister," I say firmly, "Claudia is dead."

Sis wails. I feel like I am some sort of hostage negotiator, except Sister is both the hostage and the captor. "We've been over this. My name is Aura Solara Sorcerella. It's official; I have stationery. Our bathrooms are filled with ASS embroidered towels. You used them to wipe the perspiration from your forehead the last and only time you visited our tree house. Please don't backpedal. You've chosen to remain in my journey, thus my life."

"Jesus, Claudia. The court fines I paid when you lived with me during high school. That guy who set your car on fire in our driveway. After everything we've been through, some rock 'n' roll weirdo can just roll up and brainwash you?"

Sister is not receptive to meditative breathing exercises so I decide to suggest something a little more hands-on for her anxiety. "Sister, if I send you some special brownies, will you eat them?"

CT passes by with the walking stick and gives me the thumbs-up, meaning he's embarking on a defecation stroll. I wave goodbye. Perhaps sensing my tension, he jiggles his dingy slightly.

"Sweet earth for my loveworm," he shouts, "I shall return." Several flies are enjoying the streaks of grapefruit juice that ran down his chest and pooled in his groin and thighs. As he walks past me there is a loud unified buzzing; it is so cosmic, all those individual flies but just one buzz. It strikes me that it's like my feelings for Sister—all the different harsh emotions could come out in one unified primal scream. I emit this into the receiver once CT has ventured far enough on his defecation stroll that he will not hear me and fear danger has struck my physical person. CT and I do not like to use toilets—we only do this when we have to, like in super-posh hotels and backstage on television programs and concert tours. Sometimes the super-posh hotels have double toilets and then he and I sit on them together, stare at each other, and try to predetermine when the other will flush, thereby flushing at the same time without ever looking away from one another's eyes or communicating a will to do so. We have gotten very, drastically close to simultaneously flushing on more than one occasion. I'm pretty sure complete synchronicity is nigh the next time we are at the Plaza.

"You just blew my ear out. I'm hanging up."

Sister does not understand that her ears are already worthless. Their spiritual defects predated my scream by decades.

"Sis, if I want to ingest the most powerful hallucinogen the Worm Eternal has provided to earthlings and copulate with my soul mate beneath the desert stars, that is my business and my right."

"The balcony of your Vegas hotel suite is not the desert! Do you know how many photos there are of you plastered everywhere, how many videos? How is continuous sex for that long even possible? The police had to break into your room."

The psychoactive vital worm-fluid allows for radical love-energy. Management was charged for the cost of the door. "Sister, no harm, no foul."

"No HARM? You look like sex freaks to the entire world! You should see the faces you're making! Two attractive people should have better orgasm faces. You look carsick and blinded by headlights."

"It's not about how we look to other humans, Sis. Third eye. There's more to see than you think."

"Ugh, it's on the TV right now." There's a long silence; I can almost hear her eyes squinting. "What the hell is that, a tattoo?"

I decline to answer, as Sister wouldn't understand. I recently had a bottle of wine tattooed on my mons.

"CT and I got married," I offer.

Sister hangs up, then calls back and hangs up again, then finally calls back and is able to sort-of speak through the wheezing.

"Married to that creep," she sputters, "to that pervert hustler? Did you know he hit on me at Thanksgiving? I was putting the cranberry sauce into Tupperware when I felt a stiffness on my leg and turned around. He was down on the floor like a crab rubbing his . . . his . . . *extension* near my ankles. His pants were made of some weird sheer material. I could feel everything."

"He is a wonderful lover, Sis."

"I can't do this right now," she says, and then hangs up.

I stay on the phone and let the open dial tone be a sort of beacon-call, a homing signal for CT to return, bowels empty, groin hungry.

I should mention that Sister is also my mother, somewhat. When Mom died, Sister was nineteen and I was four. As a teenager I used to love calling Sister "Smother." She was overbearing, and it was a perfect combination of "sister" and "mother."

"Sustainable," replies CT, "so bitching." We've come to see Gustav, a fashion designer whose mansion is built into the side of a cave. One room of his house is actually filled with bats; when I grabbed an infrared flashlight sitting by the door and shined it up to the ceiling, there were tons of bats instead of popcorn paint. The room has no furniture due to "Ze guano, *yeesh*!, ze guano," but there is a mounted television on the wall that plays looped footage of a buxom young woman feeding a loaf of French bread to a Dalmatian dog over and over again.

We came to Gustav to get fitted for full-body leather suits. "Ju can wear zees forever," he says, "drink en zem, sex en zem, die en zem." They have zippers and ties all over the place so they can stay on during a variety of activities, like going to the bathroom or getting an immunization shot in the upper arm.

CT raises his glass of wine up to the ceiling, an enthusiastic salute. The wine is red and has ten to fifteen drops of bat blood in each bottle; it's from the designer's own vineyard with blood from his own bats.

Then CT covers his mouth with the glass and sucks in with his cheeks so the glass stays magically attached to his face as a sort of bulb-nose. He looks at the ground and puts his arms out in a crucifixion pose, then begins moving his arms and skipping around the room. He resembles a postapocalyptic hummingbird who has to fly around with its own personal glass vase of nectar attached to its face since all the flowers are dead.

Gustav disappears for a minute and then returns holding three pairs of night-vision goggles. "Let us go inside ze bat cave," he suggests. He is no longer wearing a shirt.

The goggles make everything green and give us all emerald eyes, the bats and CT and the designer. Several battery-operated floor cleaners roam around the cave's paved cement and eat the guano. They remind me of stingrays or giant moving sand dollars, very flat and white.

Gustav kneels down onto the floor and begins untying CT's new leather suit fly. I look away. "It kind of feels like we're underwater," I say, "an underwater cave." But in the cave, as in water, my voice does not seem able to travel.

For a moment there is a sting of panic in my stomach; my mellowness is suddenly a balloon full of water being poked with a stick. It could burst open or just spring a leak or perhaps not puncture at all. The free love of the Worm Eternal instructs us to love our fellow worms in communal polyamory.

But sometimes I fail the Worm and grow jealous.

CT hands me a bottle of bat blood wine. "My cherished one, please pour this on top of Gustav and me, pour it slowly so that he and I shall be like a primordial fountain flooded with the sacred blood of cursed statues, unholy stones."

And then the stick poking my balloon turns into a feather, and I am tickled. I feel my Inner Worm remind me that Intensity comes when I forget that life is art, and Intensity is what clogs the path to enlightenment. As CT likes to say, "The boy at the top of the mountain of knowledge, the one standing like a flamingo with one leg straight and one leg bent. He is a mild child."

As I ready the bottle above CT's golden locks, dead center in the middle of his part, Gustav's head lifts up and he gives a half-hearted protest, "Don't spill, ze suit, ze suit," but CT gently moves Gustav's head back downward, the way a parent might guide the cheek of a child who just had a nightmare back down to the pillow.

"How can I wear a leather suit that does not carry the stains of wine and blood?" asks CT, and Gustav does not answer; of course the question was rhetorical, and the bloody wine pouring over their green night-vision bodies fully cloaks them. I feel more powerful than ever, like a superhero who has shadow-juice as one of her many weapons. I streak their bodies with the unseen.

When my phone rings there's about a fourth of the bottle left. I tilt the bottle over CT's mouth and drizzle the rest of it inside until he makes a happy noise.

My phone's screen is so green that beneath the goggles it

seems wholly interactive. I speak to it for some time before realizing I need to press a button to answer. Luckily it's just Sister calling, and she keeps calling until I pick up. Once she tried to call when I had a few squares of acid beneath my eyelids. When I finally distinguished the source of the ringing I mistook the phone for a fetal orb—not an orb from the beginning of time but a baby orb, one that has only been alive for a few million years—so I sang children's songs to it and told it bedtime stories, hoping this would make its musical electronic cries please, please stop. I later got distracted by CT leading me to a hammock that had been stretched over a hot tub at his request by the really expensive hotel's staff, but the next morning I saw that I had eighty-seven missed calls, all from Sister.

"Hello," I say. I am unsure of the duration of time it takes me to complete the word. The bat blood wine—at least our particular serving, I am beginning to realize—has complications to its chemical makeup beyond alcohol and blood.

"Oh Lord. Are you on drugs right now? Call me back later when they wear off. This is important." I can hear sliding window blinds in the background and I know that she is staring out at the sky with a deep frown on her face.

"I'm fine," I say. "Just sleepy. Just terribly awake." I hear Sister's nervous fingers tapping on the glass of the windowpane, or maybe someone knocking on a really thick foam door. "Sister?" I ask, because it is so quiet except for the rustling of the bats and the gentle sounds of Gustav's mouth that I can't remember whether the conversation has ended and she has already hung up or not.

"Listen," she says. "I want the rest of your share of Mom's estate money. All of the little that's left. I want you to sign your half over to me. CT is rich and you don't need it. The real reason I call you all the time and ask for money is because I'm not in good health and you've been paying my doctors' bills. Sometimes I need medications badly and quickly but I feel like I have to ask you every damn time I use some of your money from the trust, and you're usually impossible to get ahold of. How can I put this delicately? I want you to give me the money so I don't have to talk to you ever again."

The electronic vacuum cleaners, perhaps detecting CT's new emission on the floor, all rush over to CT and Gustav, encircling them. It's very cute, like the two of them are surrounded by a hungry brood of flat Maltese puppies. "Mine sweet bitter fruit," Gustav is saying to CT, licking the stains of wine on CT's suit of leather.

"Sister," I say worriedly, "you are hurt? Your health is failing? We shall heal you together! We shall sail through the air like spores from a fern of renewal, a pollen containing life and promise, a seedling that blossoms into substance where before there was void!"

Sister's words take on a strained, metal colander tone; her voice is so tight that it will hardly even strum. "You don't know anything about life or trying to live," she says. "Would you like to call my insurance company and ask if they accept ferns of renewal? Wait, why am I still participating in this conversation? Tell me where you are and I'll bring the paperwork and a few things of Mom's for you to have, and that will be it for us, okay? You have no idea how long I have wished for this peace. To be able to turn on the TV and see you walking down Rodeo Drive leading a goat that you painted to look like a giraffe or whatever and hear the gossip-police screech about what a lunatic you are, and simply agree and change the channel. I can't do that now. I can't do that with you in my life; instead I have to call and try and tell you to hurry up and get the damn goat into a van or a limo or what-the-hell-ever and move away from the cameras."

"It was actually CT who painted the goat—"

"I DON'T CARE," she yells. "WHERE ARE YOU?"

I pause. I'm fearful that Sister will not be satisfied with my location.

"We are in a bat cave inside of a cave-mansion in the desert," I say. Gustav looks up at me and waves a chiding finger. "No partiez, sweezheart. I have to be up early tomorrow. My friend in Milan is getting circumcised for his fortieth birthday and he commissioned ze codpiece you saw in my studio. Zat sort of ting, you deliver zat sort of ting in person."

"It's so beautiful, Gustav! I had no idea it was a codpiece. On its stand I assumed it was some kind of ceremonial container, or an urn? For the ashes of someone really special and powerfully phallic, like your father, maybe."

"WHAT THE HELL ARE YOU TALKING ABOUT!" cries Sis, and then she hangs up.

"Ze ashes of mine father, zat is a sad story." Gustav points to the electric vacuums. "Zees hungry suckers, I love zem, I have zem swarming in every room. But when my friend knocked over zee father, zey ate him before I could find zee remote to make zem stop."

The next morning, Sister calls back. "Let's try this again," she says. "Have you emerged from the cave?"

"We're on the bus," I report. I don't remember how or why, but I know that we are. The bus-bed CT and I has is so exceptional; it looks like a large clamshell and can even shut. It's not good to shut it for the entire night, though, because then the oxygen we breathe starts to get a little recycled and we wake up with bad headaches.

"Okay," she says. Her tone implies that I am completely useless. This makes me sad, so I stare into the pearly whiteness of CT's teeth. He consciously sleeps with his mouth very open. There is a complicated wellness-reason why he does this but we've both forgotten what it is. "Where is the bus headed to?"

"I will have to let you speak to the driver, Sister." She makes a *tsk*ing sound. "Thank God," she says.

"Sister," I beg. "Please tell me what has stricken your body. Let me be a part of your detoxification."

"No," she snaps. "You are a spoiled brat with no grip on reality. We don't all have rich rock-star boyfriends. The hardest part of your day is figuring out what pills you're on." She sighs a loaded sigh; I hear leaves stirring inside of it. Very dead, very dried leaves. They scare me, these leaves inside my sister's voice.

"Let me get you the driver," I whisper.

This news about her health is stirring my eternal waters. I make a mental note that later on, I should put on the crystal helmet and get inside the sensory deprivation unit. Once Wolf Rainbow got sued because a fan in Idaho climbed aboard the bus without our knowledge, got inside the sensory deprivation unit, and was not discovered until we were in Atlanta one week later. It took him a few months to speak but when he did all he could talk about was how totally grateful he was, so his family finally dropped the charges.

"Here," I tell her, "here you go."

"Finally," she exclaims, "someone sane."

"His name is Fractyl Clymber, Clymber with a 'y.' " I tap him on the shoulder and he gives a jump and spills a large thermos of purple tea all over the dashboard. Because he is small-statured, his arms stretch wide when holding the bus's large steering wheel. This combined with the fact that his eyes aren't very open makes him look like a sleepy bird.

"Sorry," he stutters, "I thought you were something else."

"This is my sister," I say, pointing to my phone.

"My brother," he says and nods, pointing to his phone on the passenger seat. He lets out a short giggle, then looks rather distraught.

"I mean my sister's on the phone."

"Cool."

"She wants to talk to you."

The phone is down at my side, but I can hear a sound coming from it, a scream.

"If it's about *that,*" he emphasizes, "I don't know anything about *that.* Whoever did *that,* I'm sure . . . *that* was a *total accident.*"

"No, she wants to know where we're going."

"Oh." He glances across the many dials of the bus's control panel for a moment. "A sign should be coming up soon or something. These roads are totally filled with signs."

I feel Perry, CT's press agent, put his hand on my shoulder. "I'll talk to her," he says. I nod and hand him the phone.

It's daytime but the bus has heavy black curtains and tinted windows, so it always seems like the sun hasn't come up. I trod back to our bedroom. The bus's thick, shaggy carpeting is soothing on my bare feet. At almost every stop we get the carpet shampooed because none of us wear shoes when we walk around inside. It feels amazing.

I crack the clamshell open a little wider to get in and then lower its lid back down to where there's still a safe amount of sliver. When I nuzzle up to CT, his leather wine suit smells like bread. In his half-asleep state, his fingers find my hair and kind of party a little.

Moments later, there's a light knock on the clamshell. Perry slides my phone through its crack. "We're meeting her in Dallas," he tells me. I whisper thanks.

"Listen," he says.

The cracked-open clamshell bed has a crescendo effect on sound, it's even shaped like a crescendo, so when I'm inside I barely hear the first few words in someone's sentence but then the last few words are quite loud. "If you want me to deal with her for you, thAT'S FINE, SHE SEEMS REALLY ANGRY AND MAYBE . . ."

"No," I whisper. "The Worm Eternal values fortitude. I must pursue a final attempt to bring Sister enlightenment and prove my spiritual strength to the Worm Eternal." Perry pats the top of the clam.

"Okay, kiddo."

Our conversation rouses CT. He turns and puts his lips on my neck. His lips are soft as olive oil. "I was having this dream that you were a starfish and I was feeding you tempeh bacon," he says, and I shut the clam bed and we love each other; I let the whole thing with Sister be like grains of sand that just polish the softness of CT's lips even softer.

There is a slight delay in meeting the sister.

After he ate some pumpkin-flax brittle, CT's stomach got a little torn up and he requested Fractyl Clymber stop the bus for a defecation stroll.

"Not here, man," said Fractyl. "Right here is too close to *that*." But after about twenty minutes Fractyl did pull over.

We all got out and practiced yoga behind the bus while CT walked ahead. Shortly after he squatted, a sports car screeched up and a man inside the car jumped out pointing a gun.

On CT's defecation strolls, he wanders until the universe gives him a sign that he is in the right place to go. Unfortunately, this time the universe directed CT to relieve himself in the place where the man from the car's mother and sister had been hit and killed in an accident. The man kept pointing the gun at two white crosses with MOTHER and SISTER written on them, and a large plastic floral bouquet with pictures and ribbons.

CT was trying to explain himself. "Like, I detected that this was a hallowed place, man. That's why I stopped here; it was like, the earth was saying *Here, Worship Here;* I mean this is like a shrine."

"You were shitting on it!" the man with the gun screamed.

"Do you hierarchize organic matter?" asked CT. "Because I don't think that's the right way to go about things."

Just then a cop pulled up, and several minutes later a lot of photographers showed up, too. Perry walked over to me while CT was educating the cop regarding the back-and-forth of earth and man.

"You should probably call your sister," Perry said. "This is going to take a while. I don't know if we're going to make it to the show."

I decided to go ahead and dial her number, then figure out exactly what to say while the phone was ringing, but Sister picked up on the first ring.

"Sister," I began, "there has been an unfortunate detour. If the show doesn't get canceled you'll have to meet us at the arena. Tell them 'Hashish four-twenty' at the backstage area. That's our code phrase. They'll totally let you in."

"I'm not going to your boyfriend's concert and I'm not saying that phrase. What do you mean, detour?"

When the police showed up, everyone except Perry and CT, who were already talking to the man with the gun, had been forced to run inside the bus and ingest all the drugs on board. We divided them equally according to body mass, meaning Fractyl Clymber and I took the least, but it was still a pretty heavy load. Grog was already freaking out and had locked himself in the bus's closet to masturbate.

The words coming out of my mouth were like a canoe at the tip of a waterfall. I saw what was ahead but was unable to stop it. I am always for truth but with Sister sometimes the truth has to be dressed up a little bit, not hidden but wrapped up in a way that makes it better, like a Christmas present. I was feeling very chatty, though, and the sweat on my tongue didn't help. Everything just poured out.

"CT accidentally relieved himself on this grave, and now a lot of people are taking my picture." The flashes from the paparazzi's lightbulbs were bright and painful but I couldn't stop staring at them. I moved closer to the flash. "I'm like a moth or something right now," I told her. She started crying and then Perry grabbed the phone and told me to get a full-body cape for CT from the bus closet. CT was so into sharing the truth of the Worm Eternal that he had not yet proceeded to tie up the bottom and fly of his leather suit.

"Grog's in the closet masturbating," I told Perry. "He's really freaked."

Perry sighed and nodded. "You stay put. I'll get it."

When we finally arrive at the arena, the noise of the crowd doing the Howl of the Wolf is deafening. Their pack call drowns out the opening band, an experimental metal group that heavily utilizes electric bongos.

The arena's head of security approaches us. He's shivering with fear. "You've got to get out there," he pleads to CT, his voice trembling. "I've never seen a crowd get this crazy, and I've worked this arena for almost thirty years."

CT throws off his cape and uses his arm to make a sweeping motion, like he's violently clearing a table. "No problem," he says, "this is my gig, man. Don't even worry." The fly of his leather suit is still open as he walks onstage; he tends to forget about things like that, but there is no time. Also, since the crowd is already worked into such a manic rage, what better to satiate them than the sight of CT's loveworm? It is like his music: hard yet soft.

CT's voice bleeds through the loudspeaker.

"People of Earth: I come to you as an ambassador . . . from the planet of ROCK!"

With that, Grog slams the bass and the drums are off and running like a wild, hungry dog.

Let me tell you about the sound of Wolf Rainbow.

It is loud but it is a very harmonious loudness. It is like the most beautiful woman in the world beating you up with her hair.

At Wolf Rainbow concerts, I curl up in a little ball like I'm trying to keep myself from vomiting. But what I'm really trying to do is hold on. When I hear CT's voice going up through the clouds and then back down and up again at a dizzying rate, like an airplane showing off, I can't help but feel that I'm suspended on the edge of a cliff or somewhere similar where the beauty before me comes with the price of danger. A lot of people who know about the over-edge view from the top of a bridge or tall building are dead, because they climbed up in order to jump off. Sometimes I'm afraid of such ledges. I worry the view might be so beautiful as to urge me—that I might suddenly be so overcome by what a wide, big net beauty is that I want nothing more than to jump into its middle. That's how I feel about Wolf Rainbow—I'm a little afraid of falling in and losing myself.

At this moment I feel a short kick at my ribs. Sister. She must have said hashish four-twenty.

"Look at your pupils. Do you need a doctor?"

I shake my head and get up, attempting to hug her.

She steps backward and covers her torso protectively. "Please stay away. Let's just get this done. What a *complete nightmare*. Do you know that reporters get ahold of my cell phone number? No matter how many times I change it? Normally I only pick up for people I know, which is, well, you, and doctors' offices, but this time I answered every call. 'Yes,' I told them, 'I do have a comment on the latest fiasco: she and her boyfriend are crazy and I am publicly disowning her.'"

"We got married," I say. "Remember?" I would've invited Sister to the wedding if there had been time, but I didn't actually become aware of the ceremony until it had already happened. Mescaline can be that way. Grog showed me a video, though. CT and I were slathered with divine jelly and rebirthed together as twins from the Womb of the Worm.

Sister stretches out her arm, handing me a manila folder with a pen attached. "I'll show you where to sign." Suddenly she cringes and rubs her temples. The band is starting in on a particularly heavy number titled "Reign of the Pig Women." "My God," she whimpers, "do you have some aspirin?"

The Worm Eternal is wise and sneaky. He will leave you all alone on autopilot and then suddenly come back to help you when you're least expecting it. "Yes, one second," the Worm Eternal tells me to say to Sis, and then I go over to Zapruder (one of the road crew) and ask him does he have anything. I'm in luck because he just scored five minutes ago, a great score since our entire stash had to be replaced due to the cops.

Deep down, I suppose I hadn't really been dealing with Sister's request to break contact; in fact I was in denial right until the second the Worm Eternal slid into my brain. "This is your last chance," it told me. "You might never see her again if you don't do something drastic."

I return a few minutes later with a glass of cold water. "Here, Sister," I say, trying to seem nonchalant. I'm worried my voice sounds robotic since I'm being so careful with my words. I drop two pills into her hand. She's still holding her temples and cringing but when she sees the pills she cringes even more.

"Do these contain a sleep aid or something? I just want regular aspirin; I don't want to feel drowsy."

"It's regular," I tell her, "it's just from Europe. Most generic pills in Europe are neon green with a pagan star in the center."

She swallows them and opens the folder and clicks the pen above the line where I need to sign.

"Okay," I say with a nod. "I just want to read it first."

She scowls. "That's an oddly responsible thing for you to do."

I pretend to look at the words for several minutes until she leaps up off the couch, a very high leap. "Is it warm in here?" she asks. Her face and body have flushed in alarming but expected red patches and her pupils look like giant Kalamata olives. "It is," I reply, and she removes her shirt.

That's when I see that she is only wearing one breast.

I open my mouth to say something, something loving that also expresses my grief at her loss, but she's staring up at the loudspeakers.

"This is a great song," she yells, which is not what I was expecting from Sister.

"It is," I reply gingerly. "This drum solo will last forty minutes." Sister suddenly seems so changed; I'm not sure whether to talk to her in the careful way I'm used to or to just open up.

"Let's go watch them," she says. It is almost a squeal, and is total confirmation that she's most certainly in a Wormhole and I need to jump in with her. So we go to the curtain and I yell to Zapruder that she is my sister, and he checks out her boob and gives me a thumbs-up.

A few hours later we are back on the bus driving to California, and Sister is more talkative than ever. She has told us all about the cancer and her mastectomy, and when Grog says she is very doable they start flirting and take off her bra and she has Grog start drawing cartoonish flowers on her scar tissue with a Sharpie marker. She's in good spirits. It's nice to see Sister smile.

Hours later, when the curtain on Grog's bunk finally opens and the two of them come out, she's still happy, which for Sister means that she is still in a completely altered state.

"Sis," she yells, putting her naked arms around me and bringing my face to her naked chest. She rocks me back and forth like a mother for a little while.

"Tell everyone what Mom's last words were," she says. I was only four at the time but they're memorable.

"I never wanted kids." Sis completely cracks up, then I do, too. Then CT and Grog start laughing, too, and before we know it tears are pouring down our faces.

"What's this?" Sister asks Grog as he hands her the tube to a hookah, but then before he can answer she sticks it into the side of her mouth like it's that spit-sucky thing at the dentist and lets it hang out there while she continues to talk.

"You know, no offense, but I didn't want kids either. I felt like I had to take you in when she died, because Mom was such a horrible person, and I didn't want to be horrible, too. But it ruined a lot of things for me. If I hadn't been forced to grow up right then and be a parent, my life would've been much, much better."

I've known the truth of the Worm Eternal long enough to realize that Sister doesn't mean this in a personal way, that in fact the Worm Eternal has itself entered her ear and is speaking to me through her so that I will have Greater Understanding. CT gently squeezes my hand and whispers "W-I-E" into my ear, which means Wriggle-In-Effect, as in, the Worm is actively present and working.

Suddenly, the bus stops and Fractyl Clymber runs back wearing a vest of faux ostrich feathers. "Dudes, the sun is coming up and there are all these flat rocks and I think it's really cleansing. Like, I sort of took an accidental detour; I mean it's totally cool, I totally know where we are, in relative terms. But I think it was like, meant to be, because it is so fucking pure out there right now, and I think if we all just go out there and sit it'll be great, like I might even be able to forget that *that* ever happened, I mean."

When we file out of the bus, the light of dawn seems to sober Sister up a little. It's easy not to sober up in the bus-light and bus-air; the bus is sort of an intoxicant in itself. As we walk out onto the rocks Sister looks down at the light shining on her scar tissue and begins to cry.

But Grog is not about to let this happen. "Lie down, beautiful woman," he says. "Bloom like a flower." He walks to her and parts her legs with his hands and tells her to say that she's a blooming flower.

And she does. The sun is coming up brighter than I've ever seen, and it is all hitting Sister, her scarred parts and her unscarred parts, everything. And Grog's face moves into her bloom and CT walks over with his erection peeking tall and shadowy from his still-untied leather suit and he moves his face into her bloom, too, and I stretch out on a nearby rock like I do backstage at the concerts. Sister's noises are a lot like the music of Wolf Rainbow, except this time I do jump into the noise, I get lost in the sounds and become them totally. I let myself get lost inside her pleasure.

When we get back on the bus we're all pretty tired. CT and I retire to the clam bed. Sister hugs me and I hug her, too, and it's cosmic. When we hug, my boob fits into her boob-hole.

Several state lines later when CT and I wake up, Fractyl Clymber tells me that Sis asked him to let her out at the Reno airport. She left me a note saying she was going to a hospital in Arizona, and that Grog gave her a lot of money in the form of gold coins (Grog refuses to be paid in any currency but gold). She also wrote that she would call me sometime soon, or that I could call her when I was ABLE to talk. The word "ABLE" is underlined.

The biggest surprise is that she left me a white leotard. I know with one look that it was Mom's. I smell it, hoping that it will somehow still smell like her, even though she's been dead for over two decades and was mostly a horrible mom. But it smells like the bus's incense-laden air. I put it on beneath my leather suit, though. I know that soon, because of rubbing against leather all day, the leotard will acquire a very comfortable smell, like a drowsy horse.

A few weeks later we are able to stay in the hospital with Sister for a week. It's weird Worm Eternal serendipity because we were already scheduled to go to a national forest for a video shoot that was very nearby where Sister is staying. Then, during filming, the large snake wrapped around Grog's shoulders totally bit him on the johnson, just like Grog is always worried will happen to CT when we sleep outdoors. The snake's handler didn't understand it at all; she said there was no reason in the whole world why a well-fed python would suddenly bite a human, particularly in that physical region, and asked Grog what kind of cologne he uses and questions of that nature as he and the snake were being taken away to the hospital on a stretcher, which ended up being the very same hospital Sister is in.

So we canceled some tour dates so we can be here with her. I get to sit by Sister and hold her hand during and after treatment, sometimes holding her as she gets sick and leaves drops on my leather suit that are a nice type of reminder stain. And beneath the suit I always wear Mom's leotard. Late at night when the cable gets boring and Sister is asleep and CT and the rest of the gang are doing opium in the bus parked in the hospital lot ("We can do as much of anything as we want, you know? We're in the parking lot of a fucking hospital" Fractyl Clymber likes to happily declare), I often think about how family and Mother and Sister are like my suit and my leotard, skin under skin under skin, this onion whose layers can be peeled back for the Worm Eternal to help me understand. And understanding is beautiful. In fact, like Wolf Rainbow, its beauty is dizzying in fast, airplane-stunt ways: the beauty of CT's locks spiraled in a hurricane of rock music, the beauty of my sister so strong while her body is weak, the beauty of Mom's leotard becoming the color of camels and tea and milk beneath my leather suit. "The beauty beneath"; it is something I know. I say it to CT all the time now, and of course he understands. CT has always understood.

Ant Colony

When space on Earth became limited, it was declared all people had to host a complex organism on or inside their bodies. Many people chose something noninvasive, such as barnacles or a vole in a wig. Some women had breast operations that allowed them to accommodate small aquatic life within implants. But because I was already perfect-breasted (and, admittedly, vain) I sought out a doctor who, for several thousands of dollars, drilled holes into my bones to make room for an ant colony.

After being turned down by every surgeon in the book, I finally found my doctor. Actually he's a dentist. I had to lead him on in order to get what I wanted—he only agreed to do the procedure because he is in love with me.

"I have recordings of all your television appearances," the doctor told me during our first consultation, "and I own every film you've been in. I think you're the most perfect woman in the world."

Since bone ants had never been attempted, I was a study trial. My participation in the experiment had a lot of parallels to modeling, which I used to do before acting. Once a month I went into a laboratory and removed all my clothing. This latter step probably wasn't necessary, but I did it because I was grateful, and also because it was interesting to feel someone looking at my outsides and my insides at the same time. When I lay down onto an imaging machine and the doctor pushed certain buttons, he could see all the ants moving around in my body, could even zoom in on individual ants and watch them carrying around in their mandibles what he said were synthetic calcium deposits. The ants were first implanted within my spine, where their food supply was injected monthly, but they quickly moved throughout the other various pathways that had been drilled into my limbs and even my skull.

The ants' mandibles were the only part of the insects that disgusted me; they reminded me of the headgear I'd had to wear with my braces in grades six through eight. I'd refused to wear it to school or even walk around the house when I had it on. Instead I wore it for two hours each night before bed, and I spent this time reading fashion magazines with my bedroom door locked. I wouldn't allow anyone, even my mother, to see me. She used to stand at the door and beg for a kiss goodnight. This was before she got sick—she had already been dead for several years by the time the organism hosting movement started. When she began dying I didn't want to watch; I usually grew angry when she'd ask me to come see her in the hospital. The disease overtook her body until she looked parasitic herself. Near the end, if I felt her lips on my cheek while I was hugging her I'd pull away—I knew it was ridiculous, but I was afraid she might somehow suck out some of my beauty.

"Can you feel them inside you?" As he watched the scan from an outside control room, the doctor would whisper into a microphone that I could hear through a headset earpiece. His voice sounded sweaty. "Does it seem like your blood is crawling? Does it tickle? Are you ticklish?" He'd ask me questions the entire time, but even if I were to answer, there was no way for him to hear my response.

In truth I didn't feel a thing; it was hard to believe they were even there. On my first follow-up visit I made the doctor show me footage of myself in the large ant-imaging machine to prove they were actually inside me. But after a while I got used to the thought of their presence and even started speaking to them throughout the day. The doctor said this was healthy.

"It's not uncommon to feel a shift of identity," he assured me. "It's okay to talk to your organism, and to feel like it understands you. It's now a part of your self. We could talk about this more over dinner?" But I never crossed the line into dating.

Then one day I received a frantic call.

"Come in immediately," he said. "Leave the minute you hang up the phone."

At the moment, I was in the middle of shooting a commercial for a water company. He didn't care.

"What we have to discuss is far more important," he said.

I was used to people feeling like they were more important than me, but less beautiful. I often felt that every transaction in my life somehow revolved around this premise.

Defying his orders, I finished the water shoot. "Refreshing," I said. It was my only line in the commercial, and I'd been practicing all day.

I can tell you this: I did love how invisible the ants were. They were creatures that seemed to consider themselves neither important nor beautiful. Earlier that month, the doctor had given me a videotape of several ants feasting on the corpse of an ant that had died in my femur. This cannibalism was an aberration, he'd pointed out: ants do not normally eat other ants from their own colony. The doctor said he'd worked with an entomologist to specifically breed a contained bone-ant species that would eat the dead, lay the eggs in the dead, and make the dead a part of the living.

When I finally arrived the doctor was very upset—he'd canceled everything and had been waiting in his office, which is covered with wall-to-wall pictures of me, for hours.

"Your left wrist."

I slipped off my glove and held it out to him in a vulnerable way. My wrist was smooth and fragrant and had a nicotine patch on it; the doctor had suggested I quit smoking for the health of the ants. I squeezed my eyes to look beneath my skin for them. "It's like they're not even there," I muttered.

"Grip my fingers," he said, holding two of his own upon my pulse. I found this a little difficult to do.

"Oh," he said. Even though his voice sounded worried, he seemed a little pleased. "Goodness."

He ran from the room, flustered. And there I sat alone, or not alone truly.

"We seem to be in crisis," I muttered to them, and put my glove back on. Sometimes, although I know the ants aren't visible, I still get paranoid that people can see them through my arms. Wearing gloves helps.

"We are all certain this can be resolved." Seated around the table were several new doctors I'd never met, or maybe they were dentists. I spotted a magazine that I was in—mascara ad, page seven—lying on an end table in the conference room. Somehow this made me feel safer, more of a majority. There were two of me in the room and only one of everybody else.

My doctor passed me a glossy picture: its subject was an engorged ant that was either eating or throwing up—I couldn't tell which. The ant was surrounded by small piles of powder that, when magnified, looked like crumbs of bread. I gagged a bit. "Why are you showing me this?"

"This is their queen," he said. The doctor's pupils had dilated to a width universally associated with panic. "She wants you gone." His fingertip moved from pile to pile on the glossy photo, leaving a print upon each one. "These are piles of your bone. You are being devoured by the ants that live inside you."

"Eaten from within." A dull woman at the very end of the table repeated this in a parrot-like manner. She wore a large dome cap, the obvious fashion of one hosting an organism on her head. Hers appeared tall and slightly conical; I was very interested in what type of creature it might be, but it is considered rude to ask about other people's organisms—they are ultimately too personal, too much of a bodily function.

"But we feed the ants so they don't have to eat me. I come here once a month so you can put in their food."

An authoritarian doctor whispered something to my doctor, who whispered to me. "They're not eating it anymore."

I whispered back to him. "Can we start feeding them something tastier? A different bone-substitute? Real ground bones from animals? Or maybe even dead people?" I knew it was a tasteless suggestion, but I did have money and my life was apparently in danger. The authoritarian doctor scooted back in his rolling chair and looked at his shoes.

In the following weeks, my strength and health deteriorated until I was finally admitted to a very special hospital ward. It was a room my doctor had built onto his existing home, just for me.

Around this time, the doctor also started wearing a large sack around his waist—to conceal his organism, I assumed, whatever it might be. It must've grown larger since we'd first met. I was grateful my organism wasn't making me wear a sack around my waist, even if it was eating me alive. The sack made a swishing noise when he walked; in motion the doctor sounded like a giant broom.

This swishing became more and more of a comfort as I gradually lost my vision. The doctor reminded me that when one door closes another opens, and this was true; I did seem to be gaining a sort of ant-sight. My ears began to turn away from human sounds as well, but soon I could pick up more ant noises. Around the third week I asked for my room's television to be taken away. When my eyes were closed I could see various dark caves and swarming ant-limbs, and these images gradually started to feel preferential to anything I might view of the outer world.

"I'm becoming them," I said one night when I heard my doctor swish in. "I'm becoming the ants."

I heard him pull up a chair and sit down next to me. "It is wonderful, isn't it? My sweethearts, my pets?"

He hadn't called me those things before, but I was in no condition to disagree. My arms and legs could no longer move—I could only move through the ants. It was like having hundreds of different hands. I could make them go anywhere and do anything inside my body; I'd even started eating with them. Though I didn't necessarily want to devour my own bone, I had an insatiable hunger, and there was a commanding voice, *Eat, Walk, Lift, Chomp*. It was my own voice but more powerful, echoing and confident, like my home was a large auditorium and I firmly believed in everything I said. I seemed able to express only one word at a time, but this felt more liberating than restrictive—suddenly every word could be a full representation of myself.

I lost all need for time. Eventually I was certain of only two things: my appetite was getting out of control, and my old eyes were completely gone.

"The rest of the world thinks you died," the doctor told me. As he swished into the room, there was the sound of yards and yards of fabric being unwrapped and lifted. His words seemed round with satisfaction. "You cannot see it, but I have just unveiled the gateway."

I would've answered him, but I was no longer sure if my voice still made a sound or if words even came out when I felt like I was talking.

"It's right here on my waist; I've been making paths inside of me just as there are paths inside of you. After you came to see me, I began reporting to the government that I, too, hold ants inside my body, but I don't. Not yet. It is your ants I'm after. You have become the ants who ate you; your consciousness is united with theirs. And when you all crawl inside of me, we will all become one forever." As his voice continued I could feel the ants rallying, see their legs beginning to kick with heightened motion. "I never actually fed the ants you've become. I simply allowed them to eat you whole. But you will not eat me. I will feed you all properly so that you don't. We will share my stomach—I've inserted a tube whereby everything I swallow will also be accessible to you, to your thousands of minions that are now you entirely and do your bidding. I have always loved you, and when you came to my office, I knew this was the way to make you mine."

And then I smelled something irresistible and began to crawl toward it, into the new pink-gray cave that must be the doctor. If what he said was true, I was somewhat grateful to get inside of him—if my body was now just thousands of swarming ants, I certainly did not wish to be seen.

Once we had transferred, I was pleased to realize that I could see through the doctor's eyes in addition to those of my ants. It is calming to look through the eyes of another person. It stills your own thoughts almost to a halt.

"Do you love me?"

The doctor likes to ask this; he does so almost every hour. Although I cannot speak, he always looks into a mirror afterward and smiles and says that he loves me, too.

Throughout the day I have all types of sensations. Some are good, others worry me, but my fears can't grow so big that they reach outside of his body. Nothing can move beyond this body, so in a way I feel like I am the world, and he is the world, the same way that lovers feel. "How strange," I often think, though I try not to let him hear me thinking it, "to have so much in common with an unattractive man."

And then there is the evening, when sunlight pours into the window like nectar. He sits down to the dinner table, again in front of a large mirror—I think so that I can see him, though maybe he has figured out a way to see me. Then he carefully opens the bag of sugar with a knife. When I hear this sound, each of my ants jumps and he smiles, his legs and arms contract whether he likes it or not. And though they are his own, I feel as if I guide his fingertips, that the tiniest of my workers go down into the marrow of his thumb and help to grip the teaspoon.

I love watching him eat. Teaspoon after teaspoon disappears into his mouth; his saliva coats the spoon's surface with stuck granules that change its color from silver to a crusty white. I cannot decide if he did me a favor or if I'm a victim. When I try to think, all I can feel is the sugary fluid, and a rage that comes when after our feedings I still find myself hungry.

Knife Thrower

"The ghost is friendly," says Grandmother. She pushes me inside, throws in a loaf of bread, and locks the vent.

There is a strange ghost in the air-conditioning duct and it's my job to find and tame it. I did not volunteer. It is more of an assigned position.

"Hello?" I call softly. Hopefully, the ghost is Mother. Grandmother killed her a few years ago and has feared her haunting return ever since.

Both Mother and Grandmother were knife throwers by trade. Grandmother trained Mother from an early age, as Mother trained me, as Grandmother continues to train me now that Mother is gone.

▬

"Just you wait," Grandmother warned the day we lugged Mother's burlap-wrapped body out to the woods. I kept hitting up against rocks in the dark and collecting large bruises. "She'll come back and give me my what-for. I won't know a moment of peace until I die."

I dug until the sun began to appear and Grandmother's head finally peered over the hole's rim. Her normally tight bun was loose and wild; wisps of hair floated around her face like thin smoke. "Come up," she said, lowering down a rope for me to grab so I wouldn't get her hands dirty. Once I filled the hole back in, Grandma's composure returned.

It was not how I had pictured my mother's funeral.

Afterward Grandma handed me a large, glowing cigar and patted my thigh. She has a scar on her thigh from when Mother dared her to put a lit cigar there for a whole minute. I worried it was my time to receive a matching scar, but she said nothing more, so I sat by her and tried to puff until I got sick and vomited.

"Hello?" The ghost does not answer my hellos, so I take out a piece of bread and try to shape it like a ghost, then lay it in my lap like a sign. Ghosts Welcome. Ghost Spoken Here.

There is banging as Grandma hits the vent with a broom handle. "I don't hear anything," she says. "You must wrestle the ghost and win." There is more banging and then she goes to boil tea.

At night the ghost has been making rattle noises that sound like music for people who have never heard music, or people who are very lonely for sound. Grandma suspected vermin—she has caught hundreds of raccoons in her lifetime—but then one night she saw a blue glow coming from the vent.

From the sounds of the television drifting into the vent from the living room below, I can tell that it is evening. When ghosts come.

There is a saying Grandma has, "Fit in or else you'll be sorry." All I really know about ghosts is "Boo." I whisper it at first; I want to fit in but I'm also not sure what this word means to ghosts. Then I say it a little louder.

Suddenly a wind takes up all my different hairs. The hair on my head starts whipping about in sections that look very much like snakes, so much like them that I grow afraid of my own hair. My eyebrows and the soft hairs on my cheeks begin to tickle. On my arms and legs, the hairs stand straight up and prick out into my clothing. The hairs bruise and balloon. One hair in the back of my head swells out too much and pops. Injured hair is a strange sensation.

As the wind grows stronger, I start to worry: What if saying "Boo" is like swimmers cutting themselves in a sea of sharks? Maybe ghosts smell sounds, and "Boo" is the strongest scent they know. Large dust bunnies fly past me, now and again a small roach, then just one very fearful old mouse that probably came up into the vent to die and did not count on this at all. He whirls past so quickly that I barely get to see his expression, his lint-covered whiskers, but he looks tired and terrified.

I close my eyes when tiny particles of dust in the fast wind begin to sting. I can no longer hear the television, just the top of the wrapper on the loaf of bread buckled between my knees flapping back and forth. I try to think about my bed, which is soft and has a canopy that Grandmother makes fun of. But I like it. Lying beneath it, I feel like I'm a doll who someone loves.

The wind stops suddenly. Afterward, I squint for several minutes in case it starts up again. Whenever something bad happens in my life, it's best if I don't feel relieved when I think it's over. Like how we buried my mother, and now the house is haunted.

Then I feel her breath on my eyelids.

Mother. She's not as beautiful as I remember; her skin has sores and a tooth is missing. Mother's stab wounds trickle blood continuously. They are the only part of her that appears to be alive.

I forget everything I've said to her in the quiet beneath my bed's canopy since she's been gone. Our hands try to come together but they are like the ends of magnets. I cry a little and Mother starts crying, too, but this makes her blood fountain much swifter so we stop.

"Grandma did this to you."

"We had a disagreement. Don't hold it against her. When I think about it, she was right."

I remember that night. They were fighting about tequila. "It's been you, then? Haunting the house?"

"I'm sorry. When you're a ghost, not haunting is like trying not to laugh. It tickles and pushes until it hurts. Of course there are a lot of boring ghosts who find it easy not to haunt. In the afterlife, so much is boring." She tilts her head and looks at my neck, my chin. "You're getting beautiful. Hector would be proud."

Hector is my father. I remember him running away from our home when I was very little, and Mother running after him, throwing knives.

We stare at one another. It's nice to have her in front of my eyes. It doesn't make me hurt inside the way photographs of her do.

"Dear, how about we scare Grandmother together? That way you'll be in on it, and you won't get frightened."

I shrug. Grandmother is already grumpy. "You're not the one who has to live with her," I say.

Mother smiles. "You always were very good."

The running blood bothers me. I take a piece of bread and hold it against her belly like a sponge. There is no magnet-force this time; I can feel the warmth of Mother's blood beneath the bread.

"I miss you," I tell her. I hold up another piece of bread and she pushes her nose into it like it's a mask until her imprint appears. The bread begins to take on the smell of Mother's perfume. Then we hold hands through a piece of bread. I put another piece over her chest and then put my face to it and listen for a heartbeat. Her chest sounds like the inside of a giant shell. We do this until all the bread grows thin and falls apart, then I mash its crumbs into a thick ball that smells like Mother and blood and dough.

When Mother disappears, the vent goes very dark. I tuck the dough ball into my shirt pocket and crawl toward the exit. The door must have blown open in the wind.

Grandmother is asleep in her chair next to a lit candle. "Hello," I say, and Grandmother gives a frightened gasp and opens her eyes.

"Your hair." She makes a big circle motion around her head. "It is ghost-blown."

After I nod, she asks if it was Mother. "No telling," I say. "I passed out from fear." She motions me off to bed, then her eyes move toward the vent as she lights a cigar. I run up the stairs so the smoke won't take away Mother's smell on my hands or on the bread in my pocket.

Deliverywoman

It has been a long day of intergalactic delivery, and I'm feeling a little boxed-in. Though I like the homey atmosphere of my ship's small confines, about a week into a mission the air starts to smell like recycled sock.

When my Message Station Board lights up pink, I know it's Brady, WordCalling. I've never met him, but he says he's forty-three, and early on in our talks he sent a very promising five-second video of himself tensing then relaxing his back muscles. Like me, Brady is an independent outer-space cargo transporter. We are the truckers of the galaxy.

Yet our connection runs deeper. The very first time he messaged me on SingleMingle (initially, it was a bit of a debate whether or not to look past his screen name of FluidTransfer69 and try to get to know the man within), I felt that Brady had to be a Sagittarius. That's how well we clicked. And lo and behold, when I told him my suspicion, he admitted that while his birth month technically made him a Scorpio (my astrological enemy), he was born prematurely. His true sign is indeed the keeper of my star-charted soul.

Tonight we wax intellectual for a bit before getting flirty.

FluidTransfer69: *Do u think that when we die, we will be together forever, in a type of paradise? How old do u think ur dead eternal body will look? Probably younger than u actually are, right? A hot 30? Supple 27?*

As always, I open myself to him completely.

CargoBabe: *Brady, I've thought about this a lot.*
CargoBabe: *I think, and I honestly believe this, Brady, that in the afterlife, everyone will be so extremely beautiful. Perhaps even more beautiful than it is possible to be on Earth.*
FluidTransfer69: *If u were here right now, what would u suck first?*

With Brady clearly aroused by the parallel between our love and eternity, we talk until our conversation culminates physically, at which point Brady writes,

FluidTransfer69: *Got 2 clean keyboard, bye!*

We've been chatting back and forth for several weeks now, although it seems like years because the cultivation of our bond has been so rapid. He tells me that his face is badly scarred from a fuselage accident, and that because of this he fears my disappointment and is reluctant to meet me in person. I constantly assure him his appearance doesn't matter, but he hasn't yet been able to summon up the courage. Brady's back and buttocks, however, are a source of self-pride—additional photo stills, he promises, are coming my way.

It's always hard to wake from dreams where the universe has instated a galactic monarchy consisting of myself as queen and Brady as king. In them, Brady prefers to sit on the throne and generally rule in the buff.

I roll out of bed to find that the ship's septic extrication unit has broken and the frozen waste has melted. I begin my day by mopping the thaw. Because my mop sponge is fiercely rectangular, it cannot get around the tighter edges of the file cabinet and I must reserve that job for Q-tips.

Yet it is a brighter afternoon when I sit down to find that among various junk email pyramid schemes there is also a message from Brady. I open it and see a forwarded news release.

> *Hey Babe,*
> *You reading this in a towel? Check out the second story. Apes can do everything. Ha-ha!*
> *Luv, B.*

The story, indeed impressive, involves an ape both calling for help and pumping his owner's stomach with charcoal after watching her attempt suicide for the third time. He is a helperape, assigned by the state in the absence of family funds for a more human in-home caretaker. The woman is ninety-four and deathly afraid of primates.

Yet what catches my eye is the story just below it. Justice

Freeze, a cryogenic contractor largely employed by the government's penal system, is going belly-up and holding a large auction. Several criminals whose permacapsules are programmed to not unlock for centuries are up on the auction block.

I am interested in one in particular. Below the notorious big-font names that will no doubt go into the home foyers of heavy-rock musicians, there is a smaller one, barely visible, ending a long string of nobodies.

My mother, Debbie "The Destroyer" Harlow.

Mother led a life of crime. Her real screw-up, the one that landed her 450 years, involved a large day care facility and a hidden boon of methamphetamines.

She also killed my father. He was a good man, but too talkative.

As I stare at the monitor, an antsy feeling begins to overtake me. Finally, against my better judgment, I sigh and program my ship toward the auction city's coordinates.

Upon arrival I'm given a numeric paddle. I find it eerie the way the prisoners' capsules are intermixed with used and defunct science equipment. Each capsule has a large number with a minimum bid written across the icy window in grease pen.

Lucky for me, Mother's starting bid is quite low. Freelance outer-space cargo running is a hit-or-miss trade, and this year in particular has been difficult: treatment for an antibiotic-resistant infection I picked up from a toilet seat in Goron, a dome community where I dropped off a payload of refurbished filtration equipment, racked up the medical bills. Luckily, though, this hopeless time coincided with meeting Brady. My empty glass became half-empty, which can even be seen as half-full.

I'm no delicate rose, but looking at all the frozen criminals, I start to wonder if this is such a good idea. The capsules are especially frightening. They're dimly lit and humming like vending machines.

All the high-end infamous criminals were frozen bearing menacing expressions. I wonder if they made these poses intentionally, like a funny face for a driver's license photo. A few look almost peaceful; one woman in particular has an extreme glow about her. I check the paperwork and see she's been frozen for multiple homicides.

When I finally reach Mother, I'm a little taken aback. The frozen years have not been good to her. Technically, one doesn't age while frozen, but she has clearly been through a lot. Her expression is wincing and concentrated, as if she'd been paused while taking an ardent dump. She also has what appear to be freezer-burn patches decorating her cheeks and forehead. These are especially prominent along her scalp, and look as though an irritating home-perm solution was left on far too long. Does hair freeze? Her mashed-up locks resemble a matted pompadour. Now and then I see a wisp quiver beneath the gust of the capsule's internal fan.

The auction begins with the most expensive items, and I realize I'm in for a long day. I decide to check the mobile Word-Call terminals to see if Brady is logged into the system. I'm quite nervous so I eat a few double-fudge squares and pray that he's on—only his virtual presence could give me the strength I need to abstain from stress-eating an additional twelve-pack of Galaxy Bars.

As I see his screen name I sigh with relief, so hard that I fog up the screen and have to use my sweaty palm to remove condensation with more condensation. I marvel again at how quickly we were able to fall in love. It's true—when I found "the one," I just knew it.

FluidTransfer69: *Hey, where u at? Missed our a.m. freak sesh.*

Don't get me wrong; Brady and I have discussed many complex topics, such as capital punishment (he's against). But when it comes to the finer details of our personal lives, we just haven't gotten there yet. Ours is an intense and steamy courtship with little room for conversation that doesn't make at least minimal strides toward climax.

I lie.

CargoBabe: *Sorry, I was feeling ill. Better now though. Now that you're here.*

Yet I underestimate Brady's working knowledge of my psyche, his Sagittarius command of honesty that detects when something is amiss, especially with one he truly holds dear.

FluidTransfer69: *Is there someone else?* :(

The pupils of his frown emoticon are like painful daggers to my heart. Here I am, deceiving the one I love, only to cause him agony. I decide I must come clean.

CargoBabe: *Brady, I'm not an orphan as my profile states.*
FluidTransfer69: *What r u trying to say? R u married?*

Clearly, any further delay of information is not possible. Brady needs the truth and only the truth, and as my job motto states, I Shall Deliver.

CargoBabe: *Today I'm at an auction to buy my frozen convict mother.*

As I press "Enter," I imagine this information beaming through light-years of distance to reach Brady. It's a short but difficult wait before I know relief.

FluidTransfer69: *Oh. Want 2 get dirty b4 bed?*

By the time Mother is put onto the block, the more upscale collectors have long left the building. The man to my left keeps lifting his wig and scratching his scalp with the end of his paddle.

I am the first to call Mother's bid at its minimum, and am challenged only once by an awkward but well-dressed teenager who has been making the second bid on everything and accumulating an impressive frozen army. As I raise him, anxiety floods me. In my head I've already accepted a projected scenario where he bids my mother up to an unaffordable price and I leave defeated, only to be arrested five years later for breaking into his pool house in an intoxicated attempt to reclaim her. Then his shiny cell phone goes off and he leaves.

I get my mother for minimal markup, about the cost of three days of work. That is, when there's cargo work to be had, and when misfortune does not follow my delivery mission like a love-drunk puppy.

When I get her back to the ship I decide I cannot just dive in and yell to Mother's capsule Everything I've Been Wanting To Say. The comfort level has to rise; familiarity must be reestablished and achieved. As evening sets in, I boil an insta-broth and sip it in front of her.

Although it wasn't easy to fit her capsule, fifteen by six feet, into the thirty-by-twenty interior of my ship's living quarters, I believe that ultimately it will prove to be a healing experience. I think, sometimes, that my whole life, this wandering around the universe, is really just an attempt to try to outrun her and my past. But now here she is—frozen solid and consuming a large amount of electricity just inches away from wherever I am to roam about the cabin.

The heat from my insta-broth melts the frost away from her digital lock, informing me that she has over 414 years left on her sentence. When (or if) she does finally wake, I will be so dead, and she will most likely have no idea that the majority of my adult life was spent in cohabitation with her physical being. Perhaps I'm fooling myself to think that this is any kind of personal breakthrough. To say that she is emotionally unavailable is a bit of an understatement. But really, it's my life I should concern myself with. Our relationship doesn't have to be a two-way street.

When it's time to meet Brady online, I throw a blanket over Mother's capsule. My personal life should remain private. It's been a long day, and I'm ready to lose myself to the gaping void of lust. At times I worry my relationship with Brady is too heavily dependent on the sexual, but tonight I'm grateful for its numbing opiate. Afterward, when I'm about to sign off, Brady brings up Mother.

FluidTransfer69: *So what did she do, anyway?*

I fear disclosing this information may cause him to worry about a genetic bias toward psychosis on my end, but then I remember our previous bonding experience that day.

CargoBabe: *A lot of things. She has a strong thirst for money and blood.*
FluidTransfer69: *O? Sounds feisty!*
CargoBabe: *She is fierce.*
FluidTransfer69: *So have u unthawed her yet?*

Naïve as his question is, I can't help but wonder if this is his way of telling me that he soon wants to meet not only me but also the family.

CargoBabe: *That won't happen in my lifetime. She has over four more centuries on her sentence.*

I pause, pondering how much I should express to him. It's healthy, I decide, to just say what I feel.

CargoBabe: *It's kind of a shame that I'll only get to make amends on my end. There's so much I wish I could say and have her hear.*
FluidTransfer69: *Huh.*

And suddenly, I see that it's okay. That it will all be okay because I'm not in this alone. My feelings for Brady swell and I decide to express them in a humorous pun.

CargoBabe: *Thank you for listening. I feel like our love is now light-years past what it was this a.m.*
FluidTransfer69: *Pierre is happy 2 hear that! Babe?*

Pierre is Brady's name for his penis.

CargoBabe: *Yes?*
FluidTransfer69: *Is ur mom's capsule a Digilock? Cause it's all over the Internet how to open those.*

And with that, Brady demonstrates his technical prowess by cutting and pasting a series of step-by-step instructions that could have Mother room temperature by morning.

I strap into my sleepsak with a heavy dilemma. I, and perhaps I alone, am in a unique position to understand that Mother is, on many levels, a violent predator of unthinkable proportions.

Yet I'm also her daughter. Her daughter and her only child. If I were frozen, wouldn't I want her to unthaw me if I were so capable? And what of second chances? What of personal growth and change? What of her realizing that it's me, her little daughter, but arson, drug trafficking, homicide, battery, and a variety of other mistakes caused her to miss my childhood and adolescence?

I leave the blanket on her capsule all through the night. The next morning, I meet Brady online, but I'm not interested in the hot-n-heavy. I have hard-hitting questions that need answers.

CargoBabe: *Brady, I can't believe I'm saying this, but I'm thinking of dethawing my mother.*

    FluidTransfer69: *Isn't that why you got her?*
    CargoBabe: *I didn't think it was.*
    FluidTransfer69: *Then what's the point?*

Was Brady right? Had I subconsciously been hoping that I would be able to bring her back to life all along?

    CargoBabe: *She's done some very bad things.*
    FluidTransfer69: *Well, nobody's perfect.*

I'm inclined to agree with him, although I'm not sure that using her command of martial arts to force a wooden spoon handle into my father's neck could rightly be labeled an imperfection.

    CargoBabe: *I've got to go, Brady. You may not hear from me tonight.*
    FluidTransfer69: *I'll b thinking of u!*

We give each other kissing icons; I impulsively touch the screen when his name disappears.

I remember, kind of, the movie *Frankenstein*. Or maybe I'm making this up. But I think that when the creature animates, there are lots of subhuman moans and groans. Perhaps some running around and crashing into things.

    There is no technical support hotline I can call for assistance with illegally opening my mother's prison capsule, and we're a few hours away from any medi-port. My greatest fear is that she'll wake up startled and instinctually lash out at the first organic thing she senses, which will be me.

Simply opening the capsule is easy. When the door lifts up it's quite theatrical due to the frozen smoke. I wonder if I should be recording this. It seems like something my mother, the new mellowed-out one that will take to bridge and cardigans, might want to watch alone and get a bit misty-eyed to on nights when Brady and I have gone somewhere romantic and timeless: here is where my daughter pulled me from the fog of purgatory. Here is where I achieved room temperature.

Mother's expression and skin texture looked unseemly even through the frosted glass, but without any kind of cloudy filter, she is very, very grizzled. The veins in her face are prominent and green, with a slight purple tinge I can only describe as zombieish.

My panic deepens as my eyes move toward her sharpened teeth. At least, I've always assumed she had them sharpened. As the ship's control panel lights glimmer and flick across the shiny arrowheads of her incisors, it's hard not to feel like everything about her emanates a strong *Do Not Touch* vibe.

The revitalization directions are far more involved than just popping the door open, which I'm sure often had to be done for routine maintenance. Though I don't know how much routine maintenance was given to my mother, seeing as her T-zone appears to be blistered yellow with a thick layer of permafrost. A wave of pity overtakes me, and I know what I must do. This time, things will be different: I'm an adult, I have a wonderful boyfriend, and Mother will have to be grateful that I saved her from her sentence.

I proceed with caution, first restraining her limbs with a series of athletic tube socks, which I have an abundance of. Though not because I'm a fitness enthusiast (the only activity I do on board that could be labeled cardio is scrubbing; there's not room for much else), but because I love elastic. Perhaps due to the fact that I was not hugged or encased in warmth nearly enough as a child. Perhaps due to the fact that my non-sociopath parent was murdered by the non-non.

Eventually, the fluids start kicking. I do mean this literally. Tying her up was a good idea.

The legs are the first to return, followed by the upper torso. There are lots of bubbles. The gases that come out of her have a smell somewhere between Clorox and broccoli. At first her body appears to be dancing, hippie-style in reckless abandon, too drugged out to allow for symmetry of movement and timing. These seizures then pick up the pace with chest undulations. There's a small window of time when I become afraid she will short-circuit and leave me with only the smell of burnt hair and some additional emotional baggage.

She vomits several liters of a jellied maroon substance before speaking.

"You double-crossing prick," she belches. "Give me back my magazine."

By magazine, I know she is not referring to any sort of reading material.

"Mother," I say, "it's me. You're safe. You don't need any bullets. The year is 2045."

Her eyes, perhaps, still have some ice crystals passing over the retina. Maybe all she can see is blurry light. She might even think that this is the afterlife, and I an angel.

Suddenly I feel her gaze lock upon me like the scope of a long rifle.

"It's you? You sure turned out homely."

"Mother—"

She glances around the ship's quarters before biting through her cotton fetters with rodential flair.

I can feel age-old resentments beginning to boil as I watch her rooting around my tiny cabin, likely searching for instruments to fashion crude weapons from.

"Maybe, Mom, I would live in a nicer place if I hadn't gone to a government work-orphanage at the age of nine when you were incarcerated. Not just incarcerated, frozen. Beyond writing letters, even. Did you know that they didn't even tell me you'd been frozen? For the longest time, I left mail for you on my nightstand, thinking the supervisors picked it up during our morning chemical showers. I'd get long letters back and it wasn't until you started coming on to me in them and asking me to meet you in the boiler room that I realized the janitor had been stealing my outgoing mail and taking on your share of the correspondence."

Instead of listening she's riffling through my utensil drawer. "Mother, no weapons. I mean it. I didn't have to bring you back to life."

This gets her attention. She comes over and places her fingers along my throat in a way that brings instant and absolute pain, along with the inability to move. "You're getting too big for your britches."

She then opens the refrigerator and eats for three hours straight. Around hour two I decide to go to bed. I don't say a word about how the distracting light, the wasted power, and the winded sounds of plastic condiment containers spurting their last drops are keeping me from pleasant dreams. What I do say in my head—a telepathic whisper of sorts that I hope she will hear, considering the possibility that maybe being not dead but frozen for several decades opened some window of her mind to the supernatural—is this: my britches are indeed bigger than when you last saw me, Mother. I'm now a forty-three-year-old woman with a weakness for reconstituted fudge.

I wake to Mother (nude) holding a loofah scrub (mine) and looking not so happy. She was frozen before the hydrogen ration card mandate and does not understand why the shower won't operate. Since I cannot ask for additional ration cards to support a prematurely thawed felon, I'm forced to dip into my meager stash of them. She asks how long they're for.

"Three minutes," I warn. "Don't get caught in the dry with a head full of bubbles."

She hoists up an arm that appears to be covered with sawdust. "I've got more dead skin than you've got ugly. Give me another one of those things. Three minutes isn't even long enough to sand my forehead."

I tell her, "Just this once," then when I hear the water start I put all my remaining ration cards into a front-zip stomach purse designed to prohibit pickpocketing. I bought the purse for travel, specifically for when Brady and I will honeymoon on Earth in Europe.

While Mother's in the shower, I sign on to let Brady know that I've unfrozen her.

FluidTransfer69: *U guys catching up?*

I'm a sucker for simplicity and would rather not explain that since waking, all Mother has really done is fully deplete my living quarters and put me in a choke hold.

CargoBabe: *Yes.*

That night I decide that if things are going to move forward emotionally with Mother, it is I who will need to instigate the healing process. I watch on as she uses my fold-down dinette table to practice punching through wood.

She needs no practice.

"Mother, when you killed Father, that really hurt me. Especially how I had to watch it."

"I didn't tie you up and glue your eyes open."

This is true. Mother has a way of making everyone else seem in the wrong.

"Did you miss me? All those years you were frozen?"

Mother's left cheek is somewhat illuminated by the moon, which is visible across the windshield. She's sweaty from exertion. I watch as her expression remains unchanged while her fist sails through four solid inches of oak.

It occurs to me that we're now the same age. In fact, she might be a little younger. Despite her discoloration from freezing, I have to admit that her features are beautiful. It's not something she passed on.

"Mother? Because I missed you. Sometimes I was so mad at you that I told myself I didn't miss you. I even swore that I hated you, but inside I knew that was never true, no matter how much I wanted it to be."

"I was frozen, nitwit. You can't miss people while you're frozen."

In my bunk I pull the covers up over my head and wonder if my relationship with Brady is strong enough to accelerate—to the point of me seeing his face, but also to us meeting and perhaps cohabitating.

Mother could maybe not come with me.

CargoBabe: *I know this is sudden, but I've been through a lot in the past four days and it has really made me realize what's important in life. And that's loving and being loved. I love you, Brady. I want to marry you and be with you forever. I want us to live together and to end each day in your arms. Please say you will?*

FluidTransfer69: *Get married in person?*

CargoBabe: *I know you're ashamed of your scars, but there's no shame with me, Brady. What you look like doesn't matter. You're nice to me. What we have together is something I've never known before.*

FluidTransfer69: *Will ur mom come too? I think I have room.*

I quickly peer over my shoulder to make sure Mother is still finishing her home tattoo. She's deep in concentration over an electric toothbrush motor and a ballpoint pen.

CargoBabe: *Mother will not be attending the ceremony.*

We discuss logistics. Although I want to leave this afternoon, Brady has a biohazard run to finish and only one radioactive suit. We decide on Friday.

The truth is, good things do happen to good people; sometimes it just takes a while. And bad people do get punished. Mother already got hers, sort of. She should've gotten it for longer but I wanted to give her a second chance.

The rest of the week proves to be quite a struggle. I manage to get through it only because I know that soon it will all be over and I'll be in Brady's protective embrace.

On Tuesday Mother burned my vinyl curtains to create a tar-like mixture she could huff. Once high, she insisted we have a series of home-Olympic strength competitions that included arm wrestling, leg locking, and kickboxing. These were followed by a medal ceremony in which Mother awarded herself the two remaining tin cans of food on board. I went to bed hungry. This was probably for the best because my stomach was already so full of swallowed blood.

Bored on Wednesday, Mother dislodged a ceiling panel and went up into the cabin's airshaft. She emerged adorned with several pieces of DIY jewelry she'd fashioned from rats.

Thursday was a delight of secret packing. Although most of my sparse possessions had been transformed into some type of weapon, I had been able to hold on to one pair of decent underwear, elastic still relatively sturdy, for my first meeting with Brady. That night I decided to set things as right with Mother as I could.

"Mother, I want you to know that despite all that's happened, you'll always be my mother, and I love you."

She seemed to possibly absorb this. Her fingers fidgeted with her rat-tail necklace. "I can't believe they did away with television," she said. "I really didn't see that coming at all."

I get up in the early hours of morning, dress, and start toward the exit pod. Suddenly the shadow of the doorway takes form and I feel a grave disruption in my breathing that gives way to unmistakable pain. Mother, wearing an eye patch donned for purely aesthetic reasons, is holding a homemade knife. As she pulls the blade from my chest, I see that it has been whittled from a tin pork-n-beans can. Its label is still partially on.

Knowing I have just minutes, perhaps seconds to live, I don't dabble in the muck of blame or anger. Circle of life, I decide. Mother giveth, Mother taketh away. But I can't live with Brady thinking that perhaps I'd gotten cold feet, or worse, never loved him at all. I use my last remaining strength to scrape toward the WordCall console.

To my surprise, it is already lit up. There is a message between us, except the words are not my own.

FluidTransfer69: *You better hurry up and do it. Plain Jane's getting ready to bolt.*
CargoBabe: *Consider it done. I love you, "Brady."*
FluidTransfer69: *I love you, Sicko.*

"Sorry to burst your bubble." Mother hoists me over her shoulder and begins walking. "He's a steady I met back in the pen, pre-freeze. Been in wait ever since for an opportunity to spring me. Former felons aren't allowed to buy permacapsules, so when he found out I'd be going up for auction he decided to get to me through you."

The room is starting to turn a dark shade of magenta, waving at the edges like a flag of silk. Mother lowers me down and then latches something around my wrists and neck. I realize I'm in the prison capsule.

Before closing the lid, she unzips the purse on my waist and removes all my shower ration cards. From the inside of the capsule, her voice sounds echoey and godlike.

"Don't worry, I'm freezing you, not leaving you to die. It's just a flesh wound. But a deep one. I'm going to have to dump you somewhere that no one will find you for fifty years or so, long enough for me and Skinner, or Brady, or whatever you called him, to have a nice life together without you showing up to blow the whistle."

With that, the cold smoke starts. It burns in a surprising way. The fact that this should not be happening to me, that Mother and my pretend boyfriend formerly known as Brady are bad people and I am not, doesn't provide quite as much insulation from the pain as I might like. In fact, I am very cold, so cold that no one thing can be any different from another. My thoughts and my left arm are equal-sized chunks of ice. The small window of the capsule begins to frost over and I know this is my chance: this is where I get to make the face that I will have until I wake, so I open my mouth to scream. Whoever finds my capsule needs to know: something doesn't seem right here!

But the freeze comes too fast. I see my reflection in the fogging glass, my last glimpse of consciousness, and my expression isn't the howl of someone grievously wronged. I almost look playful, like I'm sticking out my tongue. Like this painful freeze was a snowflake to catch and eat. Like my mother was just some bad medicine to swallow.

Corpse Smoker

My friend Gizmo who works at the funeral home occasionally smokes the hair of the embalmed dead. The smell does not bother him; he is used to horrible smells. He claims that after a few minutes of inhaling, moments from the corpses' lives flood his head like a movie. He won't smoke the locks of children. "I did that once," he tells me, "and I watched a dog die over and over for two days."

"What happens if you smoke the hair of the living?" I'm a little intoxicated. I like Gizmo romantically, and I wonder if rather than having to tell him he could just smoke my bangs and figure it out.

"I don't know." He shrugs. "Maybe then I'm just breathing burnt hair. Or maybe then I'd steal their memories and they'd never get them back."

Memory theft is a pleasant concept to me. I've just been through a horrible breakup with my ex-boyfriend. As it dragged itself out, I often called Gizmo at work late at night. In between tokes of hair he gave me really great advice.

The next day I decide to go to the salon and get the past fourteen months of hair chopped off. "I want the hair back," I say, holding up a Ziploc bag. Since I knew I would feel strange requesting this, I decided to go to the Save-N-Snip, where there is a large hand-drawn sign near the register that says IF WE FIND LICE WE CANNOT CUT YOU; the wording is sinister and when I leave with my hair bagged I don't feel like the oddest animal they've ever seen.

At home I worry whether other people's strands of hair got swept in with mine. Who knows what stranger's memories he could accidentally smoke and attribute to me? To be safe, I go through the baggie and take out anything even remotely straight: my hair is miles of curls.

When I show up at the morgue with the Ziploc bag and a lighter, Gizmo doesn't seem too sure.

"What if I take the wrong memories?" he asks. "What if I smoke this and then you don't even remember your name?"

"I don't think so," I say. "Wouldn't you need toddler hair for that? This hair is all memories I can stand to lose."

For a moment I ponder tricking him and pretending not to know anything right after he inhales. I could ask *Where am I?* then grab his hand with confused doe eyes.

Suddenly he gets a terrified look on his face and lowers the joint. "Have you ever owned a dog who died a slow and painful death?" Gizmo asks. "And if so, did you stand by its side the whole time in constant vigil? Because in that case we should not proceed."

"No dogs," I report. "Goldfish." I make the sound of a toilet flushing.

He nods and takes a deep inhale. My head begins to feel warm and maneuvered, like certain parts of it are getting massaged. He coughs a little. "Is it working?" I ask.

"Truffles," he says, putting his hand to his forehead like a fake psychic. "You really like truffles." I nod; they are my favorite tuber.

The contents of my head begin to fill with motion, like water is bubbling up in my ears. Tiny popping sensations start up in my skull and grow steadily crunchier. Suddenly, Gizmo's eyes change.

"Your ex is a jerk," he says. This seems right, too, but when I try to come up with a specific example why, I'm left with a vague, unscratchable tickle deep in my brain. "That moron could never have given you what you want."

All of a sudden, one of the dead bodies shakes and its hand rises up on the table. I scream and hold my bubbling head. "Don't worry," Gizmo says, "it's just a death rattle."

"Just a death rattle?" I laugh. "Do you know how disturbing that sounds?"

Gizmo, undisturbed, puffs more of my hair.

When we walk over to the rattling body, it looks vaguely familiar.

"This isn't him, is it?" I ask. "My ex?"

"No. But I can see the resemblance." Gizmo tilts his head to better stare at the corpse. "Same chin." As I admire Gizmo's hands, they take a small clump of the body's hair between two fingers. He gives me a mischievous look. "Want to see what this guy's life was like?"

I decline, for superstitious reasons. I figure there's now a memory hole in my head that might take a few days—weeks, even—to fill. I worry about some other person's memories moving in as if they were my own.

When I look over at Gizmo, he's done with my hair joint. He's staring at me now; still mischievous.

"What," I ask, "spill it." We move to a corner with a bench, and the sour smell in the air grows stronger. I put my shirt up over my nose.

"Do you think it's wrong to postpone bodies from rotting?" I ask. "Formaldehyde and all that?"

"That's what happened with you and the ex. It was going badly, but you kept holding on." His gloved hands move under my shirt a little and around my bare waist. Knowing he has just handled dead flesh creeps me out at first, but then I move closer. It's probably a nice contrast for him. After touching a dead person, my skin must seem quite special and alive. "You know," he says, "I've smoked up lots of memories of bad relationships." He takes off a glove so he can press his bare hand to my face. "I know what not to do."

The body behind us gives another death rattle. It startles me and I jump, but his hand stays on my face and I don't look away. "I've seen good memories, too, though," he continues. "I know how to be a good partner."

I expect his breath to smell awful, like burnt hair, but instead it smells like Lilac Rain shampoo. I watch the fine layer of talc the rubber glove left on his hand glitter magically in the light, and the memory-hole in my brain turns hungry, then hungrier.

Eat him with kisses, the hole says; it needs to snack on a new memory right away. So we kiss, and the weird smells of the morgue suddenly turn into something tame and slippery, something our lungs can slide over like jelly, something that can hold our hearts steady through our own quiet death rattle.

Cat Owner

I invited Eddie over for dinner as a first date. I am bad at dating, which is to say, I am bad at waiting for people to fall in love with me. What is the holdup? Where is the kink in the hose?

Tonight, I've prepared mashed sweet potatoes. I'm nervous because they look like the diarrhea of a clown.

When Eddie knocks, Baxter begins to growl. Baxter is my large cat. His thyroid condition and back paw deformity make exercise difficult. Baxter's growl is low when he initially spies danger, then it gets very high if the offender does not flee. *Your cat sounds like a Hank Williams song,* an old boyfriend once said, but he said it while leaving forever so it wasn't a compliment the way it could've been.

Tonight when I open the door, Baxter slowly crawls over to Eddie's foot and bites.

During dinner, Eddie tells me all about his job as a claims adjuster. I couldn't care less. I don't even eat because I'm planning on sex, and I don't want any sloshing in my stomach or for my mouth to taste like food instead of sex. The tricky part about having sex at my apartment is Baxter, who watches on and growls while gradually crawling toward the bed, then gradually climbing up the woolly cat ramp he uses to get onto and off of the bed when I'm not home. Once he gets to the top, he approaches me and my partner and begins with the fangs. I'm so used to the biting that it doesn't bother me anymore, not even in really sensitive areas, but past partners have freaked out at Baxter's intimidating twenty-seven-pound figure and sideways tongue, combined with the biting and growling. I should note that by the time Baxter has finally reached the top of the bed he's exhausted and his mouth is foamy. "Maybe it has mad cow disease," an old fling once suggested. "He's not a cow," I replied, but the man was adamant. "Other things get it, goats and people and all kinds of creatures"; and when Baxter bit him the man sent me a bill for several expensive precautionary vaccinations he requested at the ER after leaving my apartment. Baxter kind of looks like the cat that's printed on my checks, only much larger. My checks say, WHAT'S WITH MONDAYS? and the thin Baxter printed on them is very confused-looking with tousled fur. I sent the man the check for his medical expenses on a Saturday, specifically so he'd get it on a Monday and maybe like the joke enough to get back with me. He might call one day.

"This gravy is awesome," says Eddie. That's good news. Awesome enough to sleep with me? I want to ask, although people who have the haircut I have and wear the beige vest I wear don't say such things. My haircut looks like the wigs men don when they want to pretend they are living in the era of Shakespeare. The bangs are totally harsh. I have wanted to tell cashiers, Slit your wrists on my bangs, harlot! when they are rude to me, especially when they give me an amused look as I'm buying prophylactics. I know what they're thinking: that I have no use for them.

But I do. I've even moved Baxter's on-ramp away from the bed tonight in preparation. He will not bite Eddie again. I might but Baxter won't.

Except after dinner, Eddie stands, thanks me for a lovely evening, and says how much he's enjoying getting to know me. He will not accept drink or dessert. Turns out Eddie does not imbibe alcohol. That's okay with me, I guess: all the better for his sexual performance. Finally, I come out with it.

"I'd like you to spend the night," I say. "If you're afraid the cat will be an issue, don't worry. I've planned around him. He will not be crawling up on the bed and biting you during intercourse." I feel like showing Eddie my breasts. I want to show them to someone so badly; even lifting up my shirt in front of an apathetic but consenting stranger who makes an awful face afterward would be okay, would be better than this covered-up feeling that I have.

But Eddie itches his neck and says things are moving a little fast for him. He'd like to call it a night. We hug and I don't let go as he starts walking out, but then his pace increases and I have to.

I put on my pajamas and call a pizza delivery service. Now that I know I won't be having sex, I'm famished. I ask if they'll please bring the pizza to me in bed. "I'm too tired to come to the door," I say. The order taker seems wary but ultimately agrees to the delivery.

When he arrives, I flirt but he is not a bait-taker. I craftily lift up the sheets, readying to act shocked when my breasts "accidentally" expose themselves. But he seems to predict where things are going, drops the pizza, and exits the room before I have a chance. I get the pizza free of charge.

There's a pulling sound, quiet yet slow, and I turn to see Baxter's ramp moving back toward the bed. He is scooting it using his wide forehead. He stops once to throw up but then starts again. It is the most exercise I have ever seen him get. When he finally reaches the top of the bed, his mouth is a white sea of foam. He appears to be smiling; I watch as he lumbers to the outer crust of the pizza and takes a bite.

Cannibal Lover

I once fell in love with a cannibal on the subway. I liked his scarf and I suppose he liked something about me. Perhaps my forwardness. Our eyes locked and I immediately told him of my grandmother's painkillers, which are first class and only given to elderly individuals who are also about to perish. "If you're just old or just have a terminal illness you cannot get a prescription for these," I explained to him. "Your problems must be compound and dire." He removed his hand from the stationary pole and scratched his cheek. Something about me causes people to act itchy and uncomfortable in my presence. Perhaps my forwardness. "She never stops staring at the television. I steal them right in front of her. Maybe I should empty them into my purse in a separate room, out of respect, but I like the openness of lifting them while she's sitting next to me. That way I can tell myself that she sees what's going on and would say something if she wanted to."

I'd hopped on the subway after a day at the children's park. The park has become my favorite place to kill time because I have a lot of anxiety about dying; in fact, dying is all I think about.

But when I'm around children it seems like I will someday be able to accept my own death. I observe their natural purity, the joy they derive from grass, trees, and human company, and I realize that these things would never make me joyful. So much so that I'm probably not a real person. The only thing I ever want is for something to catch on fire, both literally and metaphorically, and in this respect my death will be the universe correcting an abnormality. I also like the park because kids are easy to watch: they're fast and loud and they never stop moving. Watching kids play is like staring at an aquarium set to "boil." Children are safe catastrophes; they strike a balance between uncontrolled and harmless in a way that automobile accidents, tornadoes, and cannibals do not. But after an hour of kids, I either get a headache or get bored.

"You steal from your grandmother to get high," the cannibal summarized, but he was nonjudgmental. His comment had the tone of an open-ended question; there was an almost therapeutic inflection in the way his pitch rose near the end of the sentence, a conversational passing of the baton.

"Pretty high." By this point I was in the cottony stage of the pills. Everything seemed very insulated and cocoon-like, particularly my ears and head. Layers and layers of distance hugged my cheeks in a tactile, present manner. This made me quite conscious of being in the subway, in a tunnel, beneath the ground. I had an irrational fear that I was spilling stuffing everywhere, like a ripped pillow, and I kept reaching up toward my head to see if anything was actually coming out.

When the cannibal placed his hand against my hip, it felt like he was touching me through a sleeping bag. I drew in close to him. For a while we pressed against one another as though we were two halves of a mold.

"This is my stop," the cannibal said, and although he did not ask me to follow him, I did. I played shadow and there was no speaking or eye contact. Even after we were in the building walking up to his apartment, he did not look back at me. He shut his door in my face but didn't lock it. So I went inside.

The smell in his apartment depended on where I was standing, but I noticed that the best-smelling place was in front of a box containing several unopened bottles of bleach. Right there it smelled like the average library, a packaged scent of collection and storage. The periphery of his living room was lined with a series of padlocked chest freezers, and the soothing way they all hummed together reminded me of a dial tone. Finally he came back into the living room and handed me a glass of water with nearly twenty very small ice cubes inside.

"I'm not used to company," he said.

The pills were beginning to wane. My nerves wanted sunglasses. I felt cranky and exposed, like when the lights come on too soon after a movie. "You don't have any furniture?" I asked. Finally I climbed on top of one of the huge freezers and sat down. My legs dangled down off the side of it like a child's. He took a sip from his glass and began crunching one of the ice cubes. I noticed he had very large teeth; they were broad and flat like white rocks. Had it not been for the humming sounds of the freezers, his chewing noises would've caused my headache to scream.

"No," he replied, "I just have a bed."

"How convenient." I swallowed a mini ice cube whole, like it was a pill. I've found that eating food as though it is medication sometimes helps me feel better. I haven't chewed a grape in half a decade.

"It's the truth," he replied. I hopped off of the freezer and went on a self-guided tour of his apartment. It was true; it was the truth.

The next morning I woke later than intended—the cannibal keeps his apartment very cold. Our sex the previous night had been truly nonverbal, and I think he expected me to leave without making future plans. "Can you get dinner Thursday, maybe?" I asked. After a few minutes he came out from the kitchen with another glass of small ice cubes. His crunches seemed like a substitution for language. "It will be fun," I insisted; "I want to see you again." Finally, through a series of subtle nods, he agreed to meet me at a steakhouse. This was a concession on my part; I'm vegetarian. But I figured he would like it—there was a real steakiness about him. His skin was nearly the color of raw meat and his teeth were so wide. Much of his life seemed to revolve around those teeth. For example, he was crazy about oral hygiene. His bathroom countertop held a rainbow of different mouthwashes. The waste in his kitchen trash can was just gum and mint wrappers padded by yards of spent floss.

As I walked into work I waved at my one direct colleague and apologized for being late. She's a dresser, meaning she selects outfits to place on the mannequins I assemble. Her nose crimpled and then her face went sour. "What's with you?" I asked. Mornings when I first come in there are strewn boxes everywhere labeled by body part: boxes of left arms, boxes of long, thin right legs. I have to assemble around seven fake people by lunchtime.

"You smell like old mushrooms," she said.

I shrugged; all I could taste were the mints I'd stolen from the cannibal's house. They were the red and white kind that reminds me of Christmas. I began building a woman from the legs up and halfway through my coworker stood next to me and sighed. "Are these even skinnier than usual?" she asked. "Soon they will be two-dimensional." I held out my arm and noticed the mannequin's thigh was the same size.

"I'm jealous of them," I said.

"They have no room for organs," she countered, but it was their lives I was jealous of—living inside a window, admired all day long. In my quest to accept that I will, at some point, die, I've noticed that a lot of people use admiration to cope with mortality. Their thought process is that if they work hard and become good at something, or famous, or even if they just live a respectable life, then they'll receive admiration from others and this will soften the ultimate blow. No one has ever admired me. Though if I spent all day inside a window getting complimented, maybe I wouldn't feel so nervous or so sad. Maybe I wouldn't steal as many pills from my terminally ill grandmother.

Our dinner was awkward. I ordered only sides and the cannibal ordered nothing at all except more water and more ice cubes. Finally the waiter began to mumble something about a minimum so I added a bottle of red wine as our main course. "I hope you're thirsty," noted the cannibal. Turns out he doesn't drink.

Halfway through my meal, I began to badger him. Wasn't he hungry? Why didn't he suggest another place if he didn't like steak?

He asked why I didn't suggest another place if I was vegetarian. "I thought you would like it," I told him. "You seem like a carnivore." Without meaning to I began drinking from the wine bottle. He wiped my mouth with a cloth napkin.

"Why are you a vegetarian?"

Normally, I avoid bringing up colon cancer on dinner dates. But he asked. "My grandmother is about to die. She may have actually died this very second. She should be at a hospice, but she refuses to go."

His face twitched a little. It was only for a second, but I caught it. His face is normally a smooth, smooth song whose lyrics do not change, so when the record skips it is very obvious. Something had transformed within his features; the shadows cast by his nose and eyelashes now fell in different places. "I can never eat in front of you," he told me. "I don't eat regular things."

I guess I laughed. I reached into my purse and dropped another pill.

"How many of those do you take a day?"

"Not your concern. What do you eat?"

"Not your concern." He took in an ice cube, then said, "People."

I can't say exactly how, but I knew he wasn't joking. Working with mannequins, I see caricatures of expressions all day. It makes me sensitive to the movements of real people's faces. I can look into a crowd and notice the ground zero for Model #2342B's smirk, or the pensive mien that inspired the vacancy behind Model #2172-00's eyes. And at that moment I saw that he was doing an exaggerated impression of a regular man having dinner in a restaurant. I laughed my best wine laugh and tried to act amused, but I couldn't fake it. There was a shift in earnestness and then I could not lose his eyes; he stared at me until I looked at him straight on with an admission that I'd understood.

Instead of feeling afraid I felt excited, like we were spies. He had just confessed a beastly secret inside a packed restaurant, and no one watching us had any idea.

On the walk home the wine began to slosh around behind my eyes like a red ocean. "I might be sick," I mentioned. We stopped in an alley and I waited for an overweight raccoon to begrudgingly saunter away before I retched.

"That creature. He seems used to avoiding the vomit of the intoxicated." In the cannibal's deep voice, this observation sounded profound.

When we were back walking at our regular cadence, I apologized. "I didn't mean to be disenchanting. Or do things like that not bother you?" I asked. "Are cannibals immune to gross?"

"Not immune at all," he said. He sounded disappointed. The rest of the walk was quiet.

Because I was unwell, he tucked me into bed in my apartment and then announced he was leaving. I grabbed his wrist and noticed how white his teeth flashed in the dark. When he opened his mouth it was like someone had turned on a small lamp. "Should I be scared? Of you?" I didn't mean to be rude; this slipped out on the tail end of a hiccup.

His hand found my own and unclasped my fingers from his wrist like they were a watch. "Are you afraid of dying?" He asked this as he started toward the door—it was a question he meant to leave with me. This reminded me of high school and the way my English teacher would always ask something very thematic and complicated just as the bell rang and his words seemed to hang in the air like a fog. I rolled over onto my pillow before sitting back up and shouting after him.

"Isn't everyone afraid?"

And this was the first and only time I heard him laugh. It was more a knowing laugh than an amused one, but its shape could be mistaken as humor. "No," he said. "There are many, many people who are not afraid at all."

We started having about two dates a week. I would have liked to see him more frequently, but this was all I got. He wasn't very forthright about the details of his schedule. Occasionally I'd ask about his plans for one of our nights apart, and he would look at me and raise an eyebrow.

Then one Wednesday he surprised me at work. Wednesday is one of the days I go to visit Grandma. "You'll have to come along," I apologized. "Just stay near the door. She won't even notice you. She probably won't even notice me."

It was the usual—I brought up her mail, entered, gave her a big kiss hello, went through her bills, wrote checks for them and stamped their envelopes. I opened the refrigerator and made sure she had enough pudding to get her through the week. Then I found my favorite bottle of her pills and put fourteen of them into my purse.

Before leaving I always grab her hand and try to direct my words past her face and skin, directly through her skull to her brain. "Goodbye, Grandma." Her glassy eyes twittered a bit. I wondered if she thought my voice was coming from the television. I hugged her and walked quickly back to the cannibal at the doorway. "Let's roll," I said.

"Are you going to introduce me?" he asked. I shook my head. "There's no point."

The moment we hit the stairs I reached into my purse, grabbed two pills, and swallowed them: immediately, before they even had the chance to start working, I felt giddy. He was walking in front of me, taking each stair with a mathematical evenness, and the opportunity to throw him off-kilter was tempting. I jumped onto his back and wrapped my arms around his neck and kissed his hair, which was short but also seemed like it had never been cut; it is naturally jagged. He reached up to his shoulders and placed his arms on mine and we went down the stairs like that. I held his strong neck and he carried me all the way to the subway, where I sat on his lap. By then the pill was working and I relaxed into his body. At our stop I made him pick me up like we'd just been married, which he did not like. But he let me hold his hand as we walked up the stairs of the subway, and then of the apartment building. I'd become used to the smell of his apartment, to the way even his water had that taste about it, a primal flavor. It was like drinking the cleanest dirt on the planet.

That night I woke up and couldn't sleep. I used the bathroom but still felt restless. The hum of the freezers seemed like an invitation. I walked out into the living room and stared at them. In the dark they seemed like large white animals asleep against the walls. The one in the back left caught my eye and I went over to explore. Soon I realized what one half of my brain wanted to show to the other: the padlock was missing.

I placed my fingertips below the seal of the freezer's lip and tried to quietly lift its lid. It was more difficult than I thought—the seal seemed to be clenching itself shut. I reasoned with it, lied; "It's okay," I whispered. "I'm not the one who normally opens you, but I have his permission."

Once it came free it was like I had uncovered a secret universe. Blue light flooded out into the room and the cold mist inside the freezer greeted me with a mysterious form of smoke. The lid instantly seemed to want to close; I felt a downward pressure that I fought against. My panic grew as I found I could not fight it back; I wasn't strong enough. It took me a moment to realize that this was due to the cannibal. He was standing right next to me, pushing down upon the lid.

"We need to talk," he said.

In my surprise I backed away from the freezer. The lid snapped shut and he immediately padlocked it. I felt a vague anger swell in my chest, upset that he had denied me. "Why can't I see?" I asked. "If it would frighten me away, do you think I'd even be here?"

His pajamas were completely white. In the dark he was simply a body with floating teeth.

"Let's go back to bed."

"No. Let's not." I felt my chest thumping and my head whining. "I'm here and I'm sleeping with you. I might love you," I said. "It isn't fair for you to have so many secrets."

"Seeing inside that freezer is very different from thinking about seeing inside."

"It won't be once you let me look."

At this point he switched on the light, but a shadow remained over his face.

"And then what? You look inside and see and then what?"

I shrugged my shoulders.

"I've been letting us pretend I'm something else."

"So we stop pretending," I said.

He shut the lamp back off and walked back to the bedroom, and I followed.

Following him wherever he went, I reminded myself, got me into this mess, but I lay down and our bodies found each other and in the morning when I woke up he was already awake and staring at me.

The next night, he did not call. When I finally broke down and phoned him two days later, his number had been disconnected. I went to his apartment and banged and banged and waited, but there was no answer.

At work, the mannequin limbs suddenly seemed unfairly heavy. I kept thinking of him off somewhere in the city, handling real body parts. My assemblage time dropped and I got behind on my quota. My coworker kept running in yelling, "I needed a body for this outfit five minutes ago!"

"I'll wear the outfit," I pleaded. "Let me pose and stand in the window." She laughed and came over to help me; we struggled to push a left arm into a left arm socket. Working together we managed to finish; I promised her I'd be better tomorrow.

That Wednesday I stopped by the supermarket and got more pudding, then went to the pharmacy to pick up Grandma's refills. I would need extra help, I knew, to get me through the week, possibly even through the month and the year.

Maybe I would sit with her and eat some pudding and take more pills and not call or show up at work tomorrow. If I got fired I could just begin sitting with Grandma all day and night. Maybe, I reasoned, the two of us had enough grief in common to live side by side.

When I opened her door, I had to step back and look at the apartment number to make sure the key had unlocked the right place. The lights were off and so was the television. Flipping on the light switch, I walked into an empty living room. She was not in her chair. On the seat there was a bottle of pills and a note written in sprawling cannibal handwriting: PLEASE POUR THESE DOWN THE SINK AND LEAVE IMMEDIATELY. GO BEGIN LIVING YOUR LIFE.

I sat down in the chair, which still had the strange odor of her sick body. The onrushing guilt of leading him to her was growing as a sticky heat in the back of my ribs. I took two more of her pills to stave it off, turned on the television. I waited for tears but felt only tranquil fatigue, a fuzziness that was massaged by the bright images of a popular cartoon. I wanted to go take something from him in return—to break into his apartment, if he even still lived there, unplug all his freezers and let their contents spoil.

It was only hours later, when the night grew dim, that I noticed his face entering the periphery of my vision. His teeth were aglow in the dark with a similar electricity as the television screen. With the TV at my feet and his vibrant teeth at my head, I found myself bookended by light. And what an insufferable anguish, to be surrounded with brightness but radiate nothing at all.

Teenager

I am sixteen years old and I cannot have Luke Gunter's baby. I have seen my older cousin's deflated football breasts. They have weird marks and lines that make them look like optical illusions, like how pencils placed into glasses of water appear broken.

Pregnancy ruined her whole body. She will tell this to anyone. She had just one kid and now her whole backside looks like a Salvador Dalí painting.

Vaginal elasticity is a secondary concern. I do not want to suffer the fate of many a cute sweater, suddenly stretched too large for proper wear. I want to keep my vag as tight a squeeze as the glove in the infamous O. J. Simpson trial.

I have a lot on my mind even before Kristi removes her left shoe.

You're missing half a toe?

Kristi is a risk-taker. She explains that one night she and her former boyfriend (his real name is something like Brian but he goes by DJ Sex, even though he's not a DJ) each made a pact to cut off a piece. Kristi, of course, went first. DJ Sex has a small machete collection thanks to the Citrus Park Flea Market, and after icing down her pinky toe she hooked it over a wooden stool. The real pain apparently came in the hours that followed. The actual moment of separation was only a pinch, like the guns they use to pierce your ears in the mall.

DJ Sex chickened out, but that isn't why she dumped him. "He started working at the gag-gift store next to Cookie Time. It was just too weird to hang out there. Every time I'd go in he and his coworkers were playing with a giant glow-in-the-dark body condom, all stoned and giggling. He seemed so seventh grade all of a sudden."

We are painting our nails. Kristi's bedspread is a cowhide rug that she's very protective of; she keeps making little "tsk" noises at me when my foot gets too close to the edge of the towel.

"I beat you," she says. With only nine toenails Kristi has an unfair advantage. "It's sort of why I never wear flip-flops. I mean I care what people think but I don't."

This is true. When Kristi was fourteen she got pregnant (pre–DJ Sex) and paid Laura Fitch's older brother Steve forty dollars to drive her to Orlando for an abortion, even though she knew he'd tell everyone.

I started hanging out with Kristi a few months later, when she got an iguana, but recently our friendship has taken an intimate and critical turn since I, too, am with fetus. "Think of it as fat and you're going to get lipo," she says.

I'm not going to just stop in at the first clinic I pass. I want to go to the Blooming Rose.

Procedures there are costly. It's not one of those clinics whose cement-block walls are covered with STD info posters (one such poster at our school gives each STD an illustrated, anthropomorphized version of what that STD might look like, were it a grumpy cartoon character. Chlamydia looks like an electrocuted gumdrop).

The Blooming Rose has Georgia O'Keeffe paintings.

Though if I put it on my credit card, my parents might see the billing statement and get *involved*. Unfortunately I didn't get knocked up by Kristi's now-boyfriend, Chet, or another student with an American Express. I'm feeling the realized danger of sleeping with scholarship recipients like Luke, even though he's totally hot and athletic, and he did get five hundred dollars for being a semifinalist when I sent his photo in to the *Teen! Teen! Magazine!* secondary school Campus Crawl contest. But that money is gone. I made him buy me a purse.

When I get home, I decide the best thing to do is borrow Grandma's credit card. She moved in with us after Grandpa died, five months before her tracheotomy. She was a model in her twenties, but she smoked like crazy and no part of her is beautiful anymore.

"Gammy, can I see your wallet a second? In Driver's Ed today they were talking about the different kinds of licenses, and how if you can't drive, they just give you an ID card. I was thinking that must be what you have. You know how you can't drive because of all the pills you take? How you hit that mail truck and they said no more wheels?" She sits up and tries unsuccessfully to straighten her wig. "Remember how you called the arresting officer a pauper in court?"

She reaches for her microphone wand. The sound used to bother me a lot, but now when she talks I just think of it as a sample in a rap song and it isn't as weird. Kristi and I told Gammy to say the word "homie" once and she did. It was hilarious.

"M-y w-a-l-l-e-t? S-h-o-o-t. M-y p-u-r-s-e i-s a-r-o-u-n-d h-e-r-e s-o-m-e-w-h-e-r-e. D-a-m-n a-l-l t-h-e-s-e K-l-e-e-n-e-x w-a-d-s. Y-o-u-r m-a-i-d t-h-i-n-k-s s-h-e-s t-o-o g-o-o-d t-o p-i-c-k t-h-e-m u-p. T-e-l-l y-o-u-r f-a-t-h-e-r t-h-a-t."

When I see her purse, I find the card and write down its numbers. She's doing something to her lapdog that seems like a tumor search, carefully rubbing little spots on his stomach.

"C-a-n y-o-u c-h-a-n-g-e m-y s-o-c-k-s? T-h-e-y a-r-e w-e-t a-g-a-i-n."

She always thinks her socks are wet. I go over and pretend I'm feeling them without actually touching her feet.

"Dry as a bone," I tell her.

Tonight Luke and I are watching TV and doing a position called "reverse jackhammer." We saw it online.

"I can really feel the blood rushing to my head!" I say. In the mirror I watch Luke's testicles bounce to and fro like a rubber cat toy. I want to reach out and bat at them playfully, except then I'd land on my skull.

When Luke finishes he always sucks in a mass of air like he just got the world's biggest paper cut. It sounds painful. The moment he relaxes, I push off his body and land back on all fours.

"That was excellent," he says. "Since we got together, I hardly watch porn."

I nod, bringing his head to my chest like he's a giant infant. He tells me all about the upcoming football game this Friday and his tactics as quarterback, who he thinks is ready and who isn't. I completely drown out the actual meaning of his words and just listen to the sound, the vibrations of it, like his voice is one of those CDs of whale calls they sell in the vitamin store.

Later I change into a sundress and go with Luke to buy muscle supplements. He's very into physical performance and doesn't drink or do drugs, but he doesn't seem to care that I do. I'm a little paranoid about this. In my worst nightmares, future Luke gets disqualified from a critical NFL game because I'm still his girlfriend and he got a contact high from my vaginal secretions and failed a pee test.

"I think you should just tell him."

Kristi and I are watching a home video of her performing fellatio on Chet. She has this idea to make instructional tapes to sell to the younger girls at school. We're trying to write notes for the voice-over narration.

"Does he dye his pubes or are they just like that?" I can't decide whether or not Chet is attractive in the throes of pleasure. His upper lip peels back from the gumline in an equine fashion. It's all very Mister Ed.

"Dunno. Maybe henna. What is so hard about telling him?"

"But I'm taking care of it." Every thirty seconds or so in the video, Kristi looks back at the camera like she's worried things aren't recording properly.

"Hey, was this on a tripod? Who taped this?"

"Levi. Look, just text him that you're pregnant. It's way weirder if he finds out afterward. Awkward."

"Levi? Your brother Levi?"

"What. I gave him twenty bucks."

"Oh, gross."

Kristi has taped nearly all her sexual exploits from the past year and a half. Anything involving threesomes with myself or another girl has the base title of "Sister Act" followed by a roman numeral.

Kristi sighs. "Luke's body is so fit. I wish Chet looked like that." This comment makes my stomach feel bad, like I've eaten too much.

Luke's *my* boyfriend, I want to say. Instead I excuse myself and go throw up. I guess it's morning sickness.

Kristi has a balloon arrangement sent to my recovery room at the Blooming Rose. One says, "You're a Star!" and is actually shaped like a star. Another, "Congratulations!"

Now that it's over with, I decide I can finally tell Luke, so I call him. But when I hear his voice I chicken out.

"Are you drunk, babe?" he asks. "You sound kind of messed up."

"I guess so," I say. He starts telling me about football practice, and I put the phone down onto the pillow and listen. A documentary about America's heartland is showing fields of sweeping wheat and grain on TV. When Luke says goodbye I make a very thoughtful noise on accident, the sound a homeless cat might make when a prospective adoptee decides against him.

I look at the balloons and decide I don't ever want Luke to know. Our relationship is a lot like a balloon, I realize. Being with Luke is so effortless. All I have to do to keep our relationship airborne, to make sure it doesn't fall on the ground, is give it a gentle tap of effort every now and then. It's so light and I want to keep it that way.

But later, when I'm cleared to check out and leave, I have this weird surge of longing for Luke. I almost can't wait to see him. I call him from the cab ride home and ask if I can stop by. I'm thinking about him holding me and the way his low whale calls will resonate with the uneasiness in the bottom of my stomach. They will cancel each other out.

People are always working on their lawns in Luke's neighborhood. I guess because they don't have people who work on their lawns for them.

When the cab pulls up to Luke's house, Luke's father is on a riding mower. I watch him for a moment, the way all his surface flesh jiggles when the mower rounds a corner. They say you can tell what women will look like when they're older because of their mothers, but I've never heard that logic applied to men and dads.

Luke and I are watching a game on ESPN in the den. I decide if his team wins, I'll tell him; if they lose, it's a secret forever. Once I have this thought, I feel like I can't undo it, even though it was a rule I made. With each touchdown Luke jumps upright to celebrate, I feel more and more terrified. My silence in the face of his excitement gets so obvious that he asks me if I'm a fan of the opposing team. It's a joke question—I've sworn allegiance to his team since we got together—but when I don't answer and forget to smile, it shakes him for a moment. "Are you?" he asks me again. He's serious.

It feels like an out that I should take: a more tolerable reason for us to break up than me telling him the truth, and the relationship getting all weighed down with feelings it can't handle.

Though of all the possible lies I could use to end things with Luke, liking another team would probably hurt him the most.

"Of course not," I assure him. He lets out the most relieved sigh I've ever heard.

"I love you," he says.

If he'd said anything else, I could've kept my mouth shut. But this was too ridiculously pretend even for me.

"You got me pregnant," I say, and he thinks I'm teasing.

"Love's just a word," he says.

"I'm serious." I take the Blooming Rose receipt out of my purse and show him. "I took care of it for us today. I know you don't have a lot of money."

"Wow," he says. On TV his team is celebrating, jumping up and down in front of the camera. "Yeah!" one of the players yells.

Luke goes completely silent. Every so often his dad rides by the window on the mower. Each time he gets to the edge of the lawn, a moment comes when if he didn't turn the steering wheel he would go off the grass and onto the road leading out of the subdivision. For some reason I keep wishing for this to happen each time. *Go*, I think. *Make a run for it.* Like the only way I can stay with Luke, in his house or as his girlfriend, is if his father goes.

I sit with Luke until the mower turns off and the garage door opens. Then, when his dad comes inside, I leave.

I decide to walk home, which is farther than I thought. I get nauseous. The thought of raiding Grandma's Marinol helps me power through.

When I finally make it there I go straight to her room.

"Gammy," I ask, reaching into her nightstand, "can I have some of those pills? The ones that make you eat ice cream? I think I got carsick."

She's asleep so I help myself. Her neck hole is breathing and making a sputtery, flapping sound. I imagine a geriatric fairy-tale scenario where she'll only awaken if the right man puts his finger into the hole and keeps it there, like a reverse King Arthur and Excalibur.

But then her eyes open, and her lips. "Gammy? I can't hear you. Use the mic."

When Grandma first wakes up she often forgets she can't talk. It's sad. It looks like she's trying to blow out thousands of candles on a birthday cake.

"I t-h-i-n-k I s-m-e-l-l c-h-i-c-k-e-n. I-t w-o-k-e m-e u-p."

"There's no chicken, Gammy." She dozes back off violently, lots of elbows, like she's being escorted to sleep against her will.

I can't help staring at her. She seems to be continually deflating from her neck hole. It looks like a withered pit that used to hold a large seed, then one day it fell out and she wilted.

It is so gross how we are born and so gross how we die.

Luke sent me a breakup text message the next day, and started dating Kristi the day after that, even though I'm sure from time to time she's still planning to use Chet as a human lollipop for continuity on her video series.

One jealous afternoon when I'm positive they're involved in an act of fornication at Kristi's at that very moment, I call Kristi's phone (knowing she will not answer) in order to get her voicemail (knowing they will listen out of curiosity, probably on speakerphone). My rage will be the soundtrack of this particular Kristi home porn session.

I leave a mean tirade about how I know they're naked together, but maybe Luke doesn't realize he's being filmed? Because Kristi's the type to just hide the camera if she's worried he's going to say no.

She begins a flurry of calls and angry texts minutes later, but I don't answer or read them. I place the phone next to my head and listen to it vibrate. If I put my ear close enough, the sound almost reminds me of Luke's dad on the riding mower. I imagine myself driving one for a minute, making circles in the grass until I get dizzy. I make myself actually dizzy doing this. An oily kind of sweetness starts to crawl up my throat and then melt back down, over and over, like something I ate long ago but am just now tasting.

Hellion

I never had breasts until I went to Hell. When I died at the age of thirty-nine I was barely an A-cup. I often used to purchase bras from the preteen section. The bra I died in had tiny unicorns patterned across one nipple and tiny rainbows patterned across the other.

As I walked around Hell I noticed all the females had them. I was looking down my shirt at them when another woman patted me on the back. "They're for defense," she said. I didn't understand until later that day when a fellow Hellion began hitting on me, a real know-it-all. The kind of person who always has a toothpick in his mouth. When I first got to Hell, I was shocked they'd let people have sharp objects like toothpicks; I expected the rules of strict prisons. But that is lesson number one. Hell is not the same as prison.

As I grew angry with the guy, my breasts began making a percolating sound. It felt like they were being forcibly tickled. My nipples hardened into nozzles and a bubbling green liquid that smelled like motor oil shot out of them. It sprayed all over the man's face and his skin began to smoke and blister.

I watched him run over to the lava pond and look at his reflection. "Now I'm a mutant for eternity!" he screamed.

A very tall man named Ben walked up and put his hand on my shoulder. Ben is intimidating at first: he is covered from head to toe with eye implants. "Sorry about that," he muttered. A bat poked its head out of Ben's beard. The bat was wearing a monocle.

Some people in Hell are nice. They just happened to have done a very reprehensible thing at one point. I killed my husband once, for instance. But I felt bad enough about it to also kill myself.

Hell isn't that awful, but it does smell. People often ask, "What died in here?"

Our currency is little coins made of hair and liver that we have to spend before they rot. We get a weekly allowance, and it's actually hard to spend it all. A lot of people start collecting things. For example, Ben collects eyes and surgically embeds them all over his body. His best eye is in his belly button. He wears little high-rise T-shirts so that his belly-eye can see and be seen at all times.

I expected a lot of axe murderers to be running around, licking bloody knives and looking sinister. But wild serial killers are totally the minority down here. Hell really isn't that violent. Maybe it's the heat.

There are a lot of people with tempers here, and a lot of nurses. I don't know why, but the bar is always full of them, guzzling fake beer and talking about how they wish they could go back to Earth for just a second and pull someone's catheter out really fast. There is only one small bar in Hell but everyone manages to hang out inside. The beer is nonalcoholic.

I was complaining about this the first time I actually got to talk to the devil one-on-one.

"You'd get dehydrated," he mumbled. "Alcohol is a great idea if everyone wants a headache."

The devil's voice isn't what you'd expect. He sounds like a leprechaun who's been smoking for centuries. The latter part makes sense—he is a smoker. Our conversation started with me telling him how exciting it was to get to smoke again in Hell. "I can't see any reason why you wouldn't," he agreed.

But newcomers experience a placebo effect in the bar during their first couple of visits, and I was no exception. As the night progressed, I started to feel intoxicated and my conversation with the devil took a turn for the worse.

"And what's up with the ceiling?" I added. "It's like the inside of the biggest dead animal in the universe." The walls are all bones and stretchy tendon.

The devil put out his cigar and stood up. "It's worked for a long time," he said. "Why change it now?" But from his expression I could tell he was hurt.

A few days later there was a knock on my door, and it was none other than the devil.

"You were right," he said and nodded, "what you said the other night."

"I was drunk," I offered. His eyebrows rose. "Though not technically."

"No, some things could be updated." We began to gaze at

one another. His eyes turned a fiery red that didn't exactly scare me but was certainly assertive.

I thought for a moment. "You could build a roller coaster?" I described my favorite ride ever, the Demon Drop, which plummets straight down and makes my stomach feel wild every time I ride it.

He agreed it would be a good thing to try. We had a raffle contest to decide the ride's name. The winner was Betty, a former Wisconsin housewife, who chose SKULLKRUSH. She seemed to hope the name would be prophetic.

As the ride was being built, the nurses wanted to know if they could set up a triage hospital next to SKULLKRUSH. "I don't think anyone will get hurt," I said, which was maybe a naïve stance about a roller coaster in Hell.

"Just in case," they insisted.

The hospital turned out to be very beneficial. The laws of physics that apply to such rides in our universe turn out to not be wholly applicable here. Of course no one can die, but mangling is very possible. On the upside, though, so is reconstruction.

Examples of this abound, like Varmint Man, who lost a rib in a poker game. I accepted an invitation from Varmint Man to try his yoga class, which wasn't the best because of the twelve baby raccoons romping around in his chest hole. Hell varmints waste no time packing up inside of cavities. They were sort of cute, but since they were demon raccoons, they had green buckteeth and pus flowing freely from their eyes.

I mentioned this to the devil one night after a wonderful date riding SKULLKRUSH (it was nice to feel the falling stomach feeling while holding his giant claw), and he was more than happy to help. He suggested we take Varmint Man dumpster diving to find something to seal up the chest hole. The dumpsters in Hell have unbelievable finds. I always thought I was hot stuff on Earth, wading through the old éclair piles behind Dough Knots. I had no idea. We ended up outfitting Varmint Man with an elaborate series of copper piping: resistant to rodent teeth. I also found an intestine that had been stuffed with rat poison and fashioned into a noose. I decided to hang the whole thing from my chandelier. "You're becoming more comfortable with entrails," the devil commented. I liked the way he took notice of my growth.

Even with the malfunctions, SKULLKRUSH turned out to be very popular. The best part was how the devil and I had succeeded in it together. "We make a good team," he said.

We were keeping the bags of profit from SKULLKRUSH at my place, but soon they started rotting. "Our money is beginning to liquefy," I told him. He tugged on his goatee for a while, seemingly weighing whether or not to say what was on his mind. Finally he sighed and took my hand and told me to get all the money together. His hands in mine gave me that great feeling of dating someone my father would completely not approve of.

We walked the bags down a long tunnel that was like an everlasting gobstopper of horrible smells: first dead cats then dead dogs then dead cows then dead whales until I couldn't even take it. "This stinks," I managed. The walls were boiling with blood.

"We're almost there." He picked me up and put me inside a pouch in his stomach that I didn't even know he had. Actually, I'm positive he just tore his flesh open and let me hang out inside so I wouldn't have to walk anymore.

The inside of the pouch was wet and oozy and took me back to when I was little. Each time my family had to go on a long car ride, my grandma first sat me down on the toilet and poured warm water between my legs to make me pee. It's something I was trained to do from the earliest age onward, and suddenly I found myself sitting in a warm blood-organ puddle. "Whatever you do," I thought, "don't pee inside the devil." I think he felt it before I did, but suddenly we both got really quiet and it was the most awkward moment of my life. Or it would've been, if I weren't already dead.

I defensively took my boobs into my hands before confessing, just in case he was sore about the whole thing. "Sorry," I offered. After it was still quiet for a moment I added, "I didn't mean to." For a second I thought I was going to faint from embarrassment but then he started laughing and so did I; I started laughing so hard that I cried. My tears were acidy and smelled like motor oil. I think my new boob ducts are connected to my tear ducts.

Finally we arrived at the end of the tunnel, where the dead smell seemed to disappear. I wriggled out of his pouch, then he reached down and did a squeegee-like wringing motion; all sorts of things splashed onto the ground and then the flap was instantly gone. It's cute how he doesn't make a big deal out of his ability to do such amazing things. Although he tells me I do amazing things that I don't think are amazing at all, like have eyebrows.

"Do you feel the air?" I asked, but he was already smiling. This was his coup de grâce.

We'd arrived at a cave where cold air was literally blasting. Feeling cold after being hot for so long hurt somewhat; it made me realize that it probably was painful to breathe for the first time when I was born. I kept breathing the cold air and soon it started to feel pleasant, like stretching a muscle that's sore.

He flipped on a light switch. In front of us there were hundreds and thousands of rows of frozen liver and hair. After stacking the bags of money in the back, he nervously put one of his arm hooves against the other and locked their grooves together. "I've never shown anyone this place before." He paused. "You can imagine how popular it would be."

"I won't tell anyone. I promise." I stretched out on a liver strip near the lip of the cave so only the top half of my body was in the freezer. I wanted to bask in the difference.

"You actually can't," he said. "I mean, you could try, but Hell won't allow you to. You'd burst into flames."

This safeguard pleased me. To be honest, I've never been able to keep a secret.

We stayed there breathing cold air for quite a while. It reminded me of the first time I smoked a cigarette. How strange it was to just breathe and feel better.

"I should be getting back," he said finally. "If I'm gone for too long, it's not good."

I nodded. Usually in Hell it's so hot that my skin is bright pink. But when I looked down I saw a very pale chest and, for the first time ever, the purple-green veins running through my acid boobs.

"You can stay if you want," he offered. "I can come get you later."

"No," I said, "I'm ready." It wasn't true. I figured he'd know that I was lying to be polite. Hopefully, this would let him know how much I liked him.

He grew wings and giant claws to hold me so the journey back would be faster.

"I love this," I said. "We should fly more often." He seemed unsure. I pressed the issue until he admitted that he doesn't like to grow wings and talons. He thinks they make his head look disproportionate. I had been pinching my nose because of the smell, but I let it go before speaking. I didn't want to sound like some annoying mother-in-law from New Jersey.

"I think you look really terrific," I whispered, and his claw tightened just a little.

Later that week he and I had such a fun afternoon that we decided to make a night of it. I tried to bake him some scones, but we got to talking and I forgot the oven and they burned. I'm horrible at baking and cooking. It was a point of contention between my husband and me before I killed him.

"Let's go back to my place," he said.

In my old life (we're encouraged to do that, to call it an "old life" rather than "life," as though Hell is still living), I did not do many exciting things. I never went on a real vacation, for instance. And I only remember swimming once when I was young. I certainly did not sleep with the devil.

"Am I going to get lucky?" I asked flirtatiously. I thought he'd like that but instead he completely clammed up.

Maybe because his house is not the Transylvanian sex-dungeon I was expecting. This isn't to say I wanted to be tortured, but moderate pain is different in Hell, less "ouch" and more "I guess I don't have anywhere else to be."

His bedroom is just really plain and ancient: a single torch and a bed. There's the usual smell of rot, but not the unbearably fresh kind. Instead it's like something died a while ago on its own and has never been found or cleaned up. Which makes me think of my husband. I imagine how much I'd freak out if the devil dragged my husband's corpse out from behind the bed, or worse, if my husband were actually in Hell at that very moment, still bearing all the death-stains I'd given him, and he'd been following me and was going to burst in during the middle of our intimate moment and ruin everything.

"I'm glad he's not here, but why didn't my husband go to Hell?" I asked. "I always thought it would be the other way around, that he'd be in Hell and I'd be somewhere else."

The devil lay down on his bed and gazed at me. I took the cue and curled up next to him.

It's amazing how perspectives can change. I was always on my husband to cut his fingernails, but the devil has the longest nails I've ever seen and they don't bother me. They're thin and very yellow—they remind me of paper in a really old book.

"Your husband was mean, but he wasn't evil." The devil's breath on my neck was hot and brothy. It felt kind of like being kissed by a pot of soup.

I stopped him for a moment, not upset but curious. "Are you saying I'm evil?"

"You did an evil thing." He said this in a fatherly and chiding way that I liked beyond words. I couldn't disagree.

When I took off my shirt he seemed to grow uneasy. For a moment I assumed it was my weapon-breasts. "Will they shoot you?" I asked. "Or do they only do that when I'm mad?"

He got up and pulled a curtain across the opening of the room, then moved toward the torch.

"Don't you want the lights out?" The way he asked this, it wasn't really a question.

"No, I want to see you." In a way, this was the biggest part of the excitement. The devil is millions of folds that I knew somehow unfold. It's impossible to describe him: he is the largest insect in the universe, and a dragon and a goat and a man and a beard and skin that has been burned clean.

"I can't," he said. "Right now, I can't."

I thought Hell would be all give or all take. But that doesn't work long-term. We're all here for eternity; we all have to go to the same small bar.

Most importantly, we all have to admit that we are wrong sometimes. Knowing there was obviously at least one time, in our old lives, when we were all very wrong makes this a little easier.

I nodded and he blew out the torch. I couldn't see him but I could feel him swelling, becoming fifty shadows almost as big as the room. My hand was on his chest when the torch blew out, and in the dark I felt his skin begin to slide under my palm like he was a magic plant growing and growing. Soon my hand was on his hip.

I began to explore his bones with my hand; I felt far more bones than legs or wings. I tried to count with my fingers their hundreds of knobs and ends. He lay back down, though he hardly fit upon the bed at this point, and coaxed me up onto him. His warm breath was coming from every direction at once.

"This part is a little normal," he said. But it wasn't true.

Afterward he fell asleep quickly. I felt him shrinking back, his entire body receding and folding, everything tucking neatly into place. I listened to the deep years of his lungs and decided to have a cigarette. We are eternal smokers, he and I.

It's true, the lighter was cheating. "Respect his wishes," I tried to tell myself. But even if it meant bursting into flames, the temptation to look was too great.

When I clicked the lighter, years seemed to pass. I could see through all the parts of him. His skin now looked like a clear bat's. In his wings, cells were beating far faster than I could see; behind his lids his pink eyes were spinning. His long tongue flickered in his mouth and his stomach was filled with what looked like small limbs.

Then he woke up and caught me peeking.

"I've been in love before," I told him, meaning the other time was not one bit like this. I felt my ribs and my stomach beginning to grow and unfold like his skin.

He shot me a smile. Don't go getting swept away, it said, a grounding look to tell me that Hell is different from my old life, but not as different as all that. Not so different that I couldn't get hurt, or hurt him. He let me look on just a moment more, then the flame was blown out by a wind that came from nowhere.

Trainwreck

Although we broke up two months ago, when he calls I agree to be his class reunion date anyway. I buy a low-cut top I can't fill and stuff it. Upon picking me up, the first thing he comments on are my breasts. They look frighteningly geometric and remind him of earmuffs, or Princess Leia.

I had cut a tennis ball in half and put one side into each bra cup. More natural-looking materials were available in my apartment, but I'd had a vision: he and I at the end of the night, drunk and reenamored. I'd take off my shirt and they'd practically glow in the dark. "Let me squeeze those fuzzy lemons," he'd say, and I'd laugh and he'd toss them across the room; we'd make love to the sounds of their bouncing.

Already it seemed that probably wouldn't happen.

When I wake up it's three thousand degrees and morning. I vaguely remember being in a large punch bowl and the DJ saying something about me over the microphone. I'm in a hot car, his, covered in a film of fruit punch and grapefruit vodka. One of the tennis ball halves is gone from my dress. I look over and see it on the driver's seat, filled with quarters next to a note:

> *Here is some change. Go wash the puke from my backseat. Please use the foam brush. The one that leaves steam lines. Everyone at the reunion asked if I'd met you that night at an AA meeting.*

I mean to do this but realize I'm so tired, so I find a flower bed a few blocks over and crash. The ants arrive uninvited. They like the dried ice-cream punch on my skin and don't stop biting if I only crush half of their bodies.

Unfortunately their carcasses stick to the punch film so I appear to have a flesh-eating disease. When I return to his car, he is standing there with a very clean woman. She is looking in at the vomit on the backseat with a glare of recollection and pain, as though it used to be her dog—her pet that somehow got liquefied and sprinkled with parsley (on the way to the reunion last night we'd stopped for some Italian. The waiter kept checking out my tennis balls).

"Are those bugs on your skin?" he asks.

"I'm Beth," the woman says, then seems instantly worried I now know her name. She can't look at me without scratching her arms. I would scratch my arms, too, but my fingernails are already filled with dead ants.

"This is your cousin?" she whispers to him.

I then realize clean Beth, likely his new girlfriend, had been unable to attend the reunion. So instead of showing up without a date he told her he'd take his cousin and called me.

When I walk up to him, Beth steps back. My one tennis boob

has fallen down somewhere in the front of my dress, poking out like the tiniest pregnancy in the world.

"That's right," I report. "We're cousins." I put my hand on his inner thigh. I realize my clothes are wet; maybe I peed myself at some point, or maybe the flower bed had sprinklers.

Beth leaves immediately, on foot.

I wait for him to run after her—to walk myself home, wash off the dead insects, and grow very, very bored.

But instead he stares. I'm itchy, squirmy; he takes it all in. His finger grazes across my ball-stomach. "I'm deciding if you're too much," he says, and I decide this is fair. I try not to scratch while I wait.

Gardener

It began during an unconscionably long dry spell in lovemaking for Robert and me. I'd gone to the bathroom to cry in my robe, which is big and towel-like and cloaks my lonely breasts that hang low from age. I kept pulling my robe in tighter to swaddle them; in my head I could hear them screaming for attention and I tried to muffle the noise through suffocation. I was pondering going into the guest room and smothering them with a pillow when I saw the gnomes.

They appeared to be necking, a female and a male gnome. I squinted at them through my bathroom window. "You're seeing things," I told myself, "that frigid man has made you lose it." Yet there they were in front of me, clearly rubbing against one another by the bushes. Then I watched the plastic deer that sits in front of our hydrangeas get up and walk over toward them, stilted on thin plastic legs, to lick the sweat from their skin.

Of course shame followed. I already felt guilty about wanting to be satisfied by my husband, who had now turned me down every night for almost half a year. Each day drew closer to that horrible landmark, the point at which, I felt, I had to accept the fact that Robert either was cheating on me or just no longer wanted sex.

But now, with these hallucinations, I had a newer, more velvet shame—was I having a psychotic break? I cannot describe how hypnotic it was to watch the gnomes, the deer with the sandpapery-plastic tongue. Whether or not I was hallucinating, watching seemed wrong at first, like getting turned on at the zoo. After the month I'd had, though, I couldn't help it. Only a few minutes passed before I opened my towel robe and pressed my flesh to the cold, dark window. Panted. Made steam.

When I went back to bed, I stared at sleeping Robert. A pie-slice-sized ray of light shone through the curtains onto his turned-up chin. My skin was flushed and my towel robe hung open, absorbing the sweat from my body. "Wake up!" I thought. "Look at me! I'm presenting you with all I have."

I said his name, shook his shoulder a little. No response.

I started to tie my robe shut, then paused. In a strange way it suddenly seemed like a door, a boundary between the fantastic and the real. Leaving it open meant a night-world where gnomes and deer lived and played. Closed meant Robert's sound snores.

For the first time in decades, I got into bed without it. I left it on the floor.

That night I had a Lilliputian BDSM dream about the gnomes tying me to my bed. It culminated with the male gnome riding in atop the large plastic deer, foreshadowing his prowess over creatures several times his own size.

I gasped as I woke, but Robert was nowhere to be found;

he'd left for work and I was stuck playing detective: searching for traces of his aftershave on the carpet in front of his dresser, looking for new stray hairs around the sink. I felt like maybe I'd invented the person I'd always assumed my husband to be, and now, at sixty-two, it was perhaps time to let the illusion go.

"Well, we're not teenagers anymore," he tells me that night in bed when I bring up how it has been six full months of abstinence. I've dressed like a cheerleader, albeit a fat, wrinkled one. I purchased the uniform from a costume shop. The fabric is cheap and the initials of the school it touts are a dubious FU.

"Do you want me to get a breast lift?" I ask, though he's already turned over and has shut off the light by his bed stand. Seeds of gentle snores are already pollinating in the back of his throat.

Against my better judgment, I creep out into the garage in my uniform.

Robert's car is a long Cadillac and I lie down across the hood and the windshield, stretching out. From here I can see the backyard out the garage's side window, and once again the gnomes have taken up one another's sexual company. The lust inside the male gnome's sturdy brow makes his cherubic face seem thrillingly dangerous. In twilight his white beard has a silvery hue; its shine is modern, like clothes the young people wear into nightclubs. He seems to be in some kind of race against himself. Or maybe it's a race against sunrise.

Spying on them, I have the strangest sensation that the car beneath me is going to start up, turn on its lights, and bust through the garage door, carrying me splayed upon it in my failed costume. Would the gnomes stop what they were doing and hide then, I wonder? Would they erotically harden in place?

The night that marked a sexless two hundred days and nights, I decided this is it. I grabbed my pillow and a blanket and left the bedroom. "What?" Robert called half-heartedly. "Is it the snoring?" I went to the guest room and told myself that from now on, I was sleeping there. I'd had enough of pretense.

The guest room is right next to the garden, so close that I feared they might see me watching. I carefully lit a single match and hid below the windowsill. Peeking through the mini blinds, I watched my gnome in the throws of passion with the yard's plumpest female milkmaid gnome. I decided that she might have to have a horrible ceramic accident soon.

But oh, his buttocks, the worker-bee industry of their contractions as they squeezed up and out! The muscles of his tiny back as he ran his fingers through her hair! I lit match after match as they burned down to my fingers, letting the pain linger slightly longer with each one. It stung: Why had I gone my whole life without knowing that kind of passion?

They finished and she fell backward into his arms, her Dutch bonnet slightly askew. He helped her step into her wooden clogs and sat back down to pack his pipe. I watched lustfully as he hitched his overalls back up. Then, suddenly, he started patting his pockets and cursing, scanning over the ground around him. It hit me: he needed a light for his pipe.

As I slid up the windowsill, I heard the collective gasp of the gnomes and other ornaments, all except my gnome, who looked at me with steady eyes. I lit a new match and held it out toward him.

When he stepped into the light of the flame, a tight grip washed through me and I felt the vertigo of six decades falling away. My mind seemed new and just-born—I could only stare at him and make heavy breaths of wonder. The creases in his forehead were so small and delicate; all his skin seemed like a soft dried fruit.

I lit his pipe but then made the mistake of grazing his forehead with my hand. He instantly turned still and cold; the fire of his pipe went to ash.

The night after this, things were different. They seemed to have moved the party underground, beneath the house. The noises were incredible. I couldn't believe they didn't wake Robert. It wasn't moaning so much as heavy construction machinery. The sounds of jackhammers and saws.

I had a hopeful theory but wouldn't let myself believe it until it actually happened: one night I woke to the guest bedroom bathed in a soft pink glow. When I got out of bed and saw his cone hat rising slowly from the ground like an emerging missile, I knew I'd been right. They'd been digging a tunnel into my bedroom floor.

All of them came in to perform for me: every ornamental animal and the swans, every gnome, even the flamingos. Of course I didn't get close or touch—I didn't want to feel like a cross between Midas and Medusa, turning them back to stone. And how awkward it would be to have to parade them all out from my bedroom back into the yard in the middle of the night, perhaps running into Robert as he headed to the bathroom with bowel trouble.

I grew and grew my collection, stopping almost daily to pick out new friends to meet in the flesh that evening. And understanding that My Gnome could not physically be mine, my jealousy faded; instead we became a team. I tried to choose the most beautiful and artfully sculpted female gnomes for him, knowing that he would trace them back to me as the root of his pleasure.

How he watched me when he was with them, and how I watched him. At first I only watched; I felt like such a simple old woman. But after a while, I began to touch myself while they played, and I watched them watch me. I felt like my desire was a giant blanket, the top of a tent, and each night they all came inside of it to move around and make me warm.

For Valentine's Day, I cooked Robert a steak to keep him busy and then told him I wasn't feeling so well. "Do you mind if I turn in a little early?" I asked. He did not look up from his potatoes, which were mashed. He was giving them a secondary mashing with his fork.

"I'm pretty bushed, too," he said.

With that, I put my dishes in the sink and ran to my bedroom. I'd gotten up early and painted togas onto all the gnomes and creatures with washable white paint—tonight I wanted a Roman theme, and they did not disappoint.

Around three in the morning I was waving goodbye as they all crawled back down into the hole, everyone except my darling. He and I had held eyes the whole night, throughout everything. "Did you enjoy yourself?" I asked, and he smiled and nodded. His rosy, tulip-bud cheeks glistened in the lamplight. Then he pointed at my braid.

My braid is long and gray; I've been letting it grow since my thirties. "You want to touch it?" I asked. "Is that a good idea?" I didn't want him to harden, though I thought of bringing him into bed in his statue form, even if he would feel like a cold doll.

At least I could put my cheek to his and sleep throughout the night.

He made a scissor motion, then pointed to the backyard and blinked. "Wait," I said. "What?" But his large knuckles just went to his lips to blow me a kiss. He walked to the magic rabbit hole they'd dug and jumped in.

I ran over and got down on my knees. But there was only carpet.

Each evening I waited for him, or any of them, to come back and answer my questions. But none of them did. I'd look out my window into the garden and he'd be there facing me, making the same scissor-shovel motions over and over. The rest of the ornaments stood behind him like disciples; with his large hat he seemed like a cult leader. They all nodded silently, appearing brainwashed.

By the end of the week, I was broken and willing to try anything. Robert was playing solitaire on the computer, generating loud, low-tech noises of victory and defeat, and I got up and ran into the garage and picked up the wire cutters. Shutting my eyes, I snipped my whole braid off below its rubber band. Wasn't that what the gnome seemed to want?

When I dangled it out before me, it did have a magic sort of look to it. Like it was the gray shed skin of a snake I'd never want to meet.

I buried the braid next to the male gnome in a shallow grave and ran back inside. "Did you get a haircut?" Robert called out, not glancing away from the computer screen.

"I did, Robert." I went into my bedroom and placed my

pillow over my face and told myself I'd nap until evening. But somehow I slept straight through: when I woke up it was already morning. My Gnome hadn't come at all.

Manic, I went to every garden center in the tristate area. I found each imaginable temptation: donkeys, centaurs, a harem of every available female gnome I could find.

When it was nine o'clock at night and all the stores were closing, I made my last purchase and handed the bills to the cashier. Unable to stop myself, I blurted out: "He has to love me. Or else I don't know what." She was young, perhaps sixteen, and chewing gum.

"I do not know anything about men," she said.

As I pulled into my subdivision, my foot hit the brake when I saw that a group of people had congregated across the street from my house. Some were pointing, others snickering. "Oh," I exclaimed when I saw it. There was a life-sized marble statue of a heavyset middle-aged man in my garden.

I ran past everyone, ignoring all the calls of my name. A miniature giraffe fell to the ground from my arms and shattered. I ran inside yelling "Robert, Robert": of course an answer didn't come. There were deer grazing around the computer where Robert had been sitting, small chipmunks outside his bedroom door.

"Oh," I cried, "oh, my." There inside my bedroom sat my real gnome in the flesh. I wish the whole world could've seen his rosy cheeks, the bedsheets turned down, his beard braided into a long braid the color and length of my former hair. I touched his bare skin and watched as it flushed and stayed soft.

Dancing Rat

I don't know if I'm able to have children. Because we haven't been able to conceive, my boyfriend calls our sex "free sex." If I ask, "What do you mean, free sex? Are you referring to the cost we save on contraceptives? To the funds it takes to raise a child?" he says, "You know. No consequences."

Kyle and I have a lot of free sex. Working on a children's TV show, I almost feel bad about how very much sex I have.

Whisker-Bop! is a musical dance program that's big on counting, manners, and household poison control warnings. I am one of the primary characters (a mouse). In addition to a small team of children, I gallivant around with a raccoon and a walrus, which is a particularly unlikely interspecies friendship. The whiskers on all of our costumes are comically long and often get in the way of things—this is one of the primary sources of comedy on the show, as is my character Sneezoid's bad allergies. In every episode I deliver multiple atch-choo punch lines in a high-pitched voice, then I look at the camera and giggle. My audition for the job almost solely consisted of me showcasing my fake sneezing abilities.

I think I took the job as a sadistic decision-making tool: Do I want a child, really, and if so do I want one badly enough to leave Kyle if he won't get more proactive? Kyle is low-key and has expressed no desire to drive to a medical plaza and ejaculate in a cup.

But the longer I'm on *Whisker-Bop!,* the less I seem to worry about whether or not to have a child, because the young "actors" I work with are horrible. Especially Missy. Her pet name for me off-camera is Ratty, though I am obviously a mouse.

Like most predators, Missy can sense fear. She reminds me a lot of Pearl in *The Scarlet Letter,* asking questions that insist she already knows more than she should.

"When you have a daughter, you won't make her do homework when she already has sooooooo many lines to memorize, will you, Ratty?"

Since day one when she asked me if I had any children and I said, "Not yet," Missy's favorite game is asking questions about my hypothetical future child that relate to Missy's own life.

"I don't know," I tell her. She then runs over to her mother yelling about how Ratty said it's unfair to make her do homework on set, and her helicopter stage parent shoots me a laser-glare.

I hate Missy but I'm also weirdly obsessed with her. She just landed a detergent commercial, and because I want to further punish myself, I probably will not be able to resist switching to that brand. I don't have a child and I probably will never have a child: I hate this but trying any harder to have one seems like it would make the reality sink in even more. It is far easier to just do the bratty things Missy asks me to do, and buy her endorsed products, and act like this agonizing relationship brings me closer to motherhood. "I am a zombie-slave under Missy's control," I often think.

The show's writers have sensed my codependent feelings for Missy. At first I was free: a free mouse. But as the episodes progressed and the show got renewed for a second season, it was decided that Missy would adopt me so that I wouldn't "have to sleep in the cold, cold fields. I think I might even be catching a cold! Atch-choo!" Those were my lines, then the two of us had a song and dance number called "I've Found My Live-In Friend."

The other children, two boys who are a bit sweeter than Missy but already vain at age seven, sometimes hear Missy call me Sneezy Ratty and try to use this name as well. I snap at them, "I'm not one of the seven dwarves."

"But Missy calls you . . ." they protest. And I just stare at them vacantly, as if to say, "Don't you get it? I'm Missy's grown-up zombie-slave."

Sometimes Kyle watches the show, even though I beg him not to. "Oh right," he says. "Like you wouldn't watch me if I was singing on television in a dancing mouse costume?"

There are moments on the show when you can actually sense me glaring at Missy through my mask, wishing her harm behind my gigantic fake eyes. All this is made worse by how incredible Missy smells—like flowers but softer, without the alcohol of perfume. Despite her evil, her smell makes me want to kiss her satin head.

Of course the home audience doesn't notice my disdain. But Kyle sees all.

"Man." Kyle laughs. "Look at your posture. You want to teach that kid a lesson."

But I do not. I want her reborn. I want her mine, without any knowledge of show business, bleached teeth, or interview skills.

Missy isn't kind or gentle. On set it's common for her to greet me by jamming her tiny fingers between my ribs and insisting she shouldn't feed her rat any more this week because I'm getting fatter. Something about Missy takes me back to high school, even though she is only six years old. Perhaps I project her popularity: she will no doubt be popular. This automatically makes her better than me, who was not even popular for a day.

Today she and I are doing a song called "Leave It Alone (If It's Under the Sink)." The dancing is strenuous, especially in the suit, where I have no sensation as to what my true range of motion is. I accidentally bounce my giant mouse midriff against her when we're doing a series of twirls.

"CUT!" Missy loves to yell this. The director and the producers have repeatedly told her that whether or not taping should halt is not her decision, but to no avail. "Fatty Ratty bumped into me!"

I give a few humble apologies through my mask, which makes a large, distorted echo inside and fills me with fears of existential loneliness.

"Take your mask off when you talk," Missy yells, "I can't understand you."

She says this despite knowing I cannot take my mask off unassisted. It is a very heavy mask with ceramic veneer on the upper face. Similar to a space suit, it screws on so that it will stay firmly in place throughout rigorous musical routines.

I put my arms up and shrug in a type of "oh well" expression. Like an abusive lover, Missy can sense when she's pushed me to the breaking point and needs to reel me back in.

"Silly mousie," she says, and then hugs me a little. I pat her tiny back with my oversized mouse paw.

"Draino? That's a big no-nooooooooo . . ." I place my paw to my forehead and spin around several times in front of a blue screen. Animated, I will appear to be swirled down an oversized sink pipe. Everything is oversized on *Whisker-Bop!* except for the children. For some reason, this makes them seem infinitely smarter.

Kyle has brought me lunch, which is our excuse to go have sex in my dressing room. I'm embarrassed that we do this near the set of a children's show, but we kind of love it and cannot pinpoint why. It's not like it even feels naughty, just creepy and a little bit pathetic.

Today, though, there are kids running through the hallway, shrieking their shrieks and banging on doors with their limbs as they pass. Though Kyle feels good, I can't help but have the children's screams redirect my thoughts to procreational aspects of sex. "There is more to life," I tell the part of my brain that wants so badly to know which one of us, if not both, is the reproductively defective one. "Pregnancy is not the goal of this sex."

But in this one moment it suddenly becomes way too much that we aren't trying to make a child. I love Kyle; at least I love a lot of him. There is enough to love there to be passed on. I want to distill us both down into seven little pounds that will grow as needed, someone who is both of us but also free of us. Someone who can give half of each of us a second chance.

"Sorry," Kyle mumbles, nuzzling his face into my chest. He's finished. I pet his damp forehead and his curly hair.

"I'm sorry," I apologize. "Sometimes it's weird for me at work."

Going back on set with fresh semen inside me reminds me of that rumor about a chemical that will turn all the water around people's legs purple if they pee in the pool. I kind of expect that one day, while walking across the Rainbow River Bridge over to the Sharing Seat, I will look down and realize my crotch is flashing like a police siren due to some product that detects seminal fluid on the sets of children's shows.

Kyle very sweetly helps redo my ponytail and screw my mask back on. The inside of the mask is disgusting; it almost looks like the hide from a real animal, or worse. I've never asked what it is. I can imagine the producer looking me straight in the eye and saying, "We recycled some old Nazi lampshades."

Kyle gives me a kiss on my mouse cheek and turns to leave when Missy appears out of nowhere like something from *The Shining*. Before she even opens her mouth I know that it is going to be horrible; I can feel the psychic energy she's drawing from my brain being sucked out the left side of my head underneath my ear.

"Why won't you give Ratty a baby?"

Kyle shoots me a betrayed look at first, and I shake my giant mouse head "No," as if to say, "Of course I never told a child your sperm might be deficient," but then reason seems to soften into him—he does know Missy, after all.

Kyle puts on a horrific fake smile that is so scary, it's like he's wearing invisible clown paint. He squats down to her eye level. "That's none of your business, is it, cutie?"

I decide it's best to intervene. "Bye, Kyle." I smile, motioning for Missy to follow me as we leave my dressing room. Missy grabs my tail a little too tightly and uses it to pull me to our start positions for the "Goodbye Should Just Be Called Catch You Later!" dance.

"What do you see in him anyway?" asks Missy. Then she laughs.

Missy's mother catches me at a weak moment. I hadn't been able to sleep all night, and around three A.M. I got up and watched a horrific birthing show on television. They showed babies coming out of crotches and then big jellyfish afterbabies, again coming out of crotches. The odd part was how I was more jealous than disgusted. I wanted to be the one screaming inside a hot tub while Kyle rubbed my back and my cartoon stomach morphed and dropped. Suddenly it was six A.M.; I'd been secretly crying since about four.

"Hello?"

Even as I picked up the phone, I wondered why I was picking up the phone; it was six in the morning. The answer, of course, was that I hoped it would be a tiny fetus calling on some human tissue receiver, asking if it could please leave its mommy and crawl into me.

"Hello?" There was a pause and then the strained voice added, "Good morning to you."

"I don't go to church." I started to hang up, but there was the sound of protest.

"No, wait—this is Mrs. Gowers, Missy's mom. I'm sorry to call so early but I have a bit of an emergency."

Apparently two of her other star children (she has three, Missy and a set of twin boys, all of them on television, all *Village of the Damned* genetically engineered–looking) had a callback and Missy's nanny was sick. "When I told Missy that I didn't know what to do with her, she specifically asked to spend the day with you." Mrs. Gowers paused. "She likes working with you, I suppose."

Mrs. Gowers does not like me. I'm not beautiful and therefore am not a good role model for Missy.

"Sure," I agreed. At first I started planning to spend the day like her mother would want us to: get mani-pedis, buy some pink things with ruffles, practice walking. But when Missy arrived she was very curious about the size of our house ("Are you poor? How poor are you? Are you ever, like, hungry but you can't eat because food costs a lot to you?"), and these questions gave me a better idea.

Munchkin Burger touts itself as "the finest mini-burger palace in the land," I tell her.

"Mom wouldn't like it if she knew I was here." Missy giggled. The skin around her mouth had taken on a greasy sheen.

"It's called pigging out," I said. This was Missy's good side. Even though I knew she would tell her mother all about it later, pretend she hated it and make me out to be a total villain, here she was: my partner in crime. Eater of the forbidden fruit.

As the day went on, my urge to defile her perfection grew extreme. I had the thought of taking her to a dive bar to see if they'd let me drink free in exchange for Missy washing dishes.

"What now?" I asked. "Television?" Missy's mouth dropped open. I suddenly realized that even though Missy is on television, she's not allowed to watch it.

"I don't want to get fat," she said. "Do you think I'm fat?"

"Do you think I'm fat?" I asked.

Missy didn't respond.

We did watch television. During each commercial, she immediately began to critique aspects of the actor's performance and physical appearance. She is completely brutal. If someone's right eye is even slightly higher than the left, she will not let this slide.

When her mother came to pick her up, Missy gave me a mini-hug, but then she ran screaming to the backseat of their deluxe SUV to see if her brothers were hired for the part. "My whole week will be ruined if they got it," she told me. Apparently the Gowers children have a competitive streak.

I watched as they drove away down the road. When her mother finds out about Munchkin Burger, she will probably make Missy get a colonic.

A few hours later when Kyle got home, the contrast was nice. Adult World. It seemed a little amusement parky—sex, alcohol, swearing. I tried to take in the sudden quiet. It was so quiet. I told myself that there was something furious and wrong about the constant sound, color, and stimulation that children crave, their habitual need to celebrate and have a party. Life is not a party. I actually said this to Kyle: "Life is not a party." I took it back as soon as I said it. It made him look sad.

"I don't get people who have children as a move toward immortality," Kyle tells me. "So that they can feel better about death or something."

I made Kyle take me to a romantic restaurant to talk about the subject. It seemed more theoretical that way, like we were making conversation rather than having a conversation. Plus, if I felt myself starting to get upset, I could take a sip of martini in a slow, calculated manner, like a robot mannequin in a commercial about robot mannequins who enjoy martinis the way real, elegant people do.

"I would like to feel better about death, though," I admit.

"It's just death. You're not going to care when you're dead."

I want to write Kyle off as a simple person, but I know him and he is not simple. It's unfair, though, how he can have so much clarity about difficult things. Why have children? Why fear death? "I mean you and I certainly don't have to have a child for the sake of our species."

"Well, Kyle, I wouldn't *want* to have a child to benefit mankind. That would take all the fun out of it." My hand finds my martini carefully, straightened, like a mission payload specialist guided it there. Grip. Sip.

"What, do you want it to give your life some kind of purpose?" He lingers on the word "purpose" and his garlicky breath finds my nose. It's a little sexy, how he smells like garlic and doesn't need a purpose.

"Well, what is life's purpose?" I cringe a little, realizing I had this conversation on one of my first dates at a coffee shop. I guess it hasn't gotten old.

"Purpose is something we think about to try to feel better about how weird everything is."

But the thought of becoming a mother is a weirdness I want to feel out a little more. I will live with it for a while longer as if it were truly a baby; I will let it grow and see what shape it takes before deciding what to do. Until then, I can go on living each day as Missy's secondary mother, a giant rodent who is slightly repulsed by her human offspring.

He and I make a toast to ourselves, to purposeless lives and our candlelit table; dinner is expensive but afterward the sex will be free.

Magician

After my older brother Keith lost his arm in a car accident, I bought him a bird. I thought it might be nice, the company and its bright color. He and I go to the same college and live down the hall from one another in the same apartment complex. We're very different, though. We did not hang out much before his accident. Keith was an athlete and an alcoholic; I prefer chemistry and yarn.

Most of the girls he hung around with were beautiful. I'm not beautiful, although he told me once that I was, kind of. "You just aren't beautiful in a way that people notice" is what he said. I don't think unnoticeable beauty is what most people are looking for. They want excitement. My face does not remind anyone of that.

When I take the bird into Keith's apartment, it's so dark that the bird stops chirping. "It is not nighttime yet," I tell the bird, but it stays quiet and does not believe me. "I brought you a bird. It will cheer you up and make you feel better," I tell Keith, but he stays quiet and does not believe me. Keith's living room is like a reverse sundial; shadows shift to tell that time does not pass.

Whenever I go over to his place since the accident, I can feel my heart breathing and my lungs beating. Things are all messed up. The pulse of my breath makes a thin white cloud in the air. The room is too cold for a bird.

I turn on the heater, and its loud ticks sound like the restoration of life. I set the bird by the window and put a towel over its cage. "It will be under there, when you're ready," I tell him. "Please do not kill it."

Keith stares at me and I realize he's looking at my sweater. "I knitted it," I tell him.

There's a moment of quiet, then he laughs a little. "You should knit something to go over the end of my arm." He smiles at my discomfort. "You should knit me a fake hand." I want to laugh, too, but laughing around Keith is like a foreign word I've forgotten the meaning of; I want to use it but I don't know how.

Keith itches the air where his arm used to be, and he and I stare at the space for a long time. Sometimes I get the feeling that everything could be okay if I could make myself touch the new end of his arm. I sit down next to him but he folds his arm into his lap. "I hate birds," he mutters.

"You'll like this one." I sound assertive when I say this, but I'm not. "I'll be able to hear it in my apartment down the hall, so we'll kind of be sharing it that way."

"Will you take care of it?" Keith asks.

For a moment I forget he's talking about the bird. I look at the dome of gauze on the end of his arm. I have a terrible urge to touch it, to pat it like the stomach of a soft doll.

"Sure," I say. We sit together until the shadows get darker but time does not pass, and eventually, gently, I place my head onto his shoulder. The end of his arm now rests so close to me that I feel like it is listening to my heartbeat. "Do you still feel your hand?" I ask. He tells me he doesn't feel anything.

A sudden chirp startles us; we'd forgotten about the bird.

I stare across the room at the towel-covered cage, and for a moment I imagine the noise as a signal for the start of a magic trick: I'll walk over to the cage and pull off the towel to reveal my brother's forearm and hand sitting inside the bars. The gauze on Keith's arm will shift and wiggle until a tiny bird pokes its way out, and then we'll both watch it fly away.

Acknowledgments

The author wishes to express deep gratitude to the editors and readers of the following publications where the stories below first appeared:

Apostrophe Cast, July 2008: "Teenager"
BOMB, vol. 113, 2010: "Cannibal Lover"
Denver Quarterly, vol. 43.3, 2009: "Magician"
Eleven Eleven, vol. 9, 2010: "Ant Colony"
La Petite Zine, vol. 21, 2008: "Bandleader's Girlfriend"
Lady Churchill's Rosebud Wristlet, vol. 24, 2009: "Corpse Smoker"
MAKE Literary Magazine, vol. 7, 2008: "Deliverywoman"
Mid-American Review, vol. 29.2, 2009: "Model's Assistant"
No Contest, October 2009: "Dancing Rat"
The Southeast Review, vol. 25.1, 2006: "Zookeeper"
Swink, vol. 3, 2007: "Porn Star"
Tin House, vol. 33, 2007: "Dinner"
Versal, vol. 5, 2007: "Trainwreck"
Quarterly West, vol. 70, 2010: "Knife Thrower"